Blessed with that Hood Love

D'Artanya

Published by T'Ann Marie Presents, LLC

Ship

"When you bringing her back?" Peaches asked as she passed me Rhea's bag.

"Either tonight or in the morning; I got something to do tomorrow." I told her, putting the unicorn bookbag on my shoulder.

"What, you got a date or something?" she asked, trying to play it off with a laugh.

"Something like that," I told her honestly.

"Oh, well excuse me." She followed me to the door.

"You excused." I stepped outside. "Give ya mama a kiss goodbye," I told Rhea.

"Bye, mommy." Poking her lips out, Rhea leaned forward, without tightening her grip on to me because she knew I wouldn't drop her.

"Bye, baby. I'll see you in the morning." Peaches kissed Rhea before looking at me.

That was her way of telling me that I was keeping Rhea for the night. I didn't have a problem with that. I could never spend too much time with her. I still hadn't adjusted to not seeing her every day, and it'd been a little over a year since I moved out.

"Don't be having no b-words around my baby," Peaches warned.

"What b word?" Rhea asked.

“Balloons,” Peaches responded. “The balloons decorated the party.”

“Girl, shut the f-word up.” I scrunched my face, walking off to my car.

“What f-word, daddy?”

“Funny, baby. Ya mama is funny.”

As many times as I'd gotten Rhea since the breakup, Peaches still was giving that warning. Little did she know, a nigga wasn't looking for love. I believed it was real; it just wasn't for me. I always wanted it more than it wanted me. Chasing after love was exhausting. A nigga was done with that shit.

Peaches was accusing me of the shit she was doing. She'd been seeing this one nigga for two months now. She thought I didn't know, but that's because I didn't care. She could pop out with a ring and quadruplets, and a nigga wouldn't feel no way about it.

“We getting ice cream, daddy?” Rhea asked as I sat her into her booster seat.

“Cake, too. Snap yourself in.”

I stood with my hand on the car door, waiting for her to snap herself into the booster seat. She made one weak attempt before giving up. She poked her bottom lip out.

“Daddy, it's too hard. I can't do it.”

I twisted my lips up at her. She was phony as shit. Peaches told me that she'd been snapping herself in and out of the booster with no problem. When her little ass got with me, she damn near forgot how to walk. I couldn't even stunt. It felt good that she wanted me to do everything for her.

“Daddy's baby safe now.” I kissed her forehead, and she cheesed, kicking her feet back and forth.

She pulled her tablet from her backpack before I made it to the driver's seat. I started the car headed for Kong's house.

To be real, a nigga wished he never got the damn test. I was happy to be done with Peaches, but every time I looked at Rhea, that zero point zero percent flashed like an open sign. After Kiss yelled the results out all ignorant and shit, I still went to look for myself. I couldn't stop staring at the motherfucker. Rhea wasn't mine. She still felt like mine, though.

It was really just me out here. Nobody to pass on the name that I got from a fucking nobody. I'll never understand why women named their children after ain't shit men. My mother knew my daddy wasn't fitna hang around. Why stamp me with his last name? Meanwhile, Rhea was living and breathing with my shit, and she was another nigga's daughter. I was starting to hate bitches.

"Ooh, daddy." Rhea dropped her tablet on the seat as we pulled up at Kong's. "Is Reagan here?" she asked.

"No, baby. I don't think Reagan is going to be around anymore." I walked around to her side of the car.

"Why? 'Cause her daddy died?" She lifted her arms so I could unsnap her from the booster.

Rhea wouldn't stop asking about Mont's daughter. Tessa wasn't fucking with us. I thought after she grieved that maybe she'd remember we were her brothers too, but she hadn't budged at all. We sent gifts for Reagan's birthday, and she sent them all back. I had Peaches reach out to her to see if Rhea and Reagan could hang, and she said no. Kiss gave Cambria some money to take to Tessa, and she turned it down. Cambria kept the shit for herself. Kiss was hot about that shit, too.

"No, 'cause her mother's a b-word," I said, lifting her into my arms before shutting the door.

"What b-word, daddy?" Rhea asked.

“Baboon,” I said. “The baboons at the zoo are misbehaved.”

That was Peaches and our thing. The both of us cursed entirely too much when Rhea first started school. She wasn’t in that Pre-K class for a whole week before the teacher called us in to talk about Rhea’s language. So, from then on, we started saying f-word and b-word. This year, Rhea was big on words, so she was asking what words we were talking about. It’d been working out to build her vocabulary up while still allowing me and Peaches to get our insults off.

“Hey, Uncle Rashawn!” Rhea ran over to Kiss.

He scooped her up and spent her around before placing her back on her feet. She took off, looking for Savon. He was three now and all over the fucking place. Kiss always had the kids, so they were always there when I had Rhea. The two of them acted like siblings. ReaLynn, who was eleven now, would ignore them with both Air Pods in her ear like a normal big sister.

“What’s good, bro?” I walked up on Kiss.

I greeted Kiss and we did our handshake. He spent the night at Cambria’s last night. I asked if he needed a ride, but he said she was going to drop him off with ReaLynn and Savon.

“Shit. Ready for them to serve this fucking food already. A nigga hungry as shit.” Kiss rubbed his stomach.

“You know black people don’t do shit on time.” I shrugged.

“Ard, y’all,” Schetta said, stepping out of the house. “Here’s the birthday boy.”

The backyard of people clapped and cheered to celebrate Saint’s first birthday. He didn’t like all the attention and burst into tears, trying to hide in Schetta’s shirt. The baby weight had done her body good. Her ass was still crazy as fuck, though.

“Stop all that fucking crying, boy,” Kong said to him.

"Shut up." Schetta slapped Kong's shoulder.

Saint was a fucking crybaby. The little nigga cried about everything. Kong couldn't stand that shit. It was funny as fuck watching this mean ass nigga be a dad. Outside of the cursing, he was doing a good job. When Schetta was at work, he wasn't calling her with a million questions. He knew all the shit that he was supposed to know. The nigga was a good daddy. He ain't have no choice 'cause me and Kiss would've been on his ass.

Kong's mother and sisters started coming out with the food. They went in and out of the house until all the food was spread across the buffet-style table.

"Come eat!" Ma called out to everyone.

"And don't be greedy either! Get a regular plate and if there's food left over, *then* you can get seconds," Whilemena called out to everybody.

We stood in line for food, and Kong walked up on us.

"Fuck all that; get what y'all want. Y'all my brothers," he said, dapping us up with our handshake.

"Hi. Rashawn." Whit cheesed in Kiss's face.

"How you doing, Whit? I like your dress," he told her.

"Thank you. It has pockets." She put her hands inside to show him.

"Ard, ard. Go find you something to do, Whit." Kong grabbed her by her shoulders and walked her away.

"I didn't say hi to Patrick, yet," she argued. "Hi, Ship." Whit waved.

"Hey, Whit. How you doing?" I asked her.

"I'm good. You?" she asked.

"You said hi. Now find somewhere to be." Kong didn't allow

her to stay for my response.

“Something really wrong with you, boy.” I shook my head at him.

“Something wrong with that nigga. Playing with my sister’s feelings and shit. He know she got a crush on his ass, and he keep entertaining her,” Kong argued.

“Boy, he just being nice. Shut the hell up,” Ma chimed in.

“Thank you, ma,” Kiss agreed. “That’s my sister, nigga.”

“Tell *her* that, shit.” Kong ran his hands down his face. “It’s hot as a bitch out here. Told Schetta’s ass we should’ve done this shit at a waterpark or something.”

“What the fuck was Saint going to do at a water park?” I asked.

“I would’ve took my lil’ man in the water. Put his ass on my lap for a few rides,” he countered.

“You’s a stupid nigga, you know that?” Kiss said.

He was making three plates. One for him, Savon, and RaeLynn. She was more than old enough to make her own plate, but Kiss was never going to stop babying her ass. I knew the feeling because I could already see Rhea being twenty-one with me still not allowing her to date.

We found a kids table and sat their plates down before calling them over to eat.

“Why I gotta sit at the kids’ table?” RaeLynn asked.

“Because you a kid,” Kiss told her.

“But she ain’t a babysitter. Y’all ain’t slick.” Ma came over. You can go on in the house and eat in the living room, baby,” Ma told her.

“Thank you, Ma Linda.”

"Ma, that's his kid. You can't be telling people what to do with their kid," Kong told her.

"She my grandbaby, and this my house. That's how it works." She walked off and we laughed.

Neither of us minded when she stepped in, and neither of us cared about the details. Belinda was my mom just as much as she was Kong's. Kiss had his mom, both his parents in fact, but he still respected Ma Linda for her role in our lives. All of our kids were her grandchildren, including Rhea. She didn't care anymore than I did that Rhea wasn't mine by blood.

With RaeLynn sent in the house, me, Kiss and Kong stood around the kids table, making sure our babies didn't choke on their food. Savon ate fast as fuck, like somebody was going to take his shit, so he had to be watched. And Rhea talked so damn much, she often skipped chewing to finish her sentence.

"You decide if you doing that *Smoke With Me* shit, yet?" Kiss asked.

"Yeah, I'ma go. They gon' toss me a little bread and I got my pick of multiple bitches, fuck it." I shrugged.

"That nigga love the fucking camera," Kong said.

He and Kiss hollered like he said some funny shit. I didn't mind the cameras. My problem was the embarrassing shit bitches did once the camera was on. Poppie played the fuck out of me, and everyone saw it. I wasn't for that shit again. But being on there, got me the little attention to be on this dating show.

Smoke With Me was a local show that often made it on The Messy Nest blog. A bunch of bitches were going to be lined up to smoke with me. I made the final decision on who I would be fucking with. Plus, they were tossing me a few dollars.

Saint started screaming to the top of his lungs. We whipped our necks to see he'd fallen off his little toy car. Schetta ran over like he'd broken a leg or something. Wynter stood there, watching the scene with one arm folded over the other, shaking her head.

Wynter still wanted her fair one with Schetta, but Kong wasn't letting it happen. So, the two of them got into it whenever they were around each other. I told that nigga to let the shit go down, so they could let their beef go. Kong was certain Schetta was going to beat Wynter's ass, and then Whilemena was going to want to jump on Schetta, too. Then, he'd be beating his sisters the fuck up. So, he wouldn't let them fight.

"You baby him too damn much, that's why he's always crying now," Wynter said to Schetta.

"And you talk too damn much." Schetta snapped on her, while bouncing Saint in her arms, holding his head to her chest. "This *my* son."

"Yeah, that all of us help you with. 'Cause if I remember correctly, I blew up all of these balloons," Wynter shot back.

"Wynter, mind your fucking business," Kong told her, even though we all agreed with her. "Give me my son," he said to Schetta. "Ain't nothing wrong with his ass." Kong took Saint from Schetta and placed him on his feet. Saint ran off, laughing, chasing after Whit, who started running to distract him.

Loud pops sounded off, and it was Schetta popping the balloons, one by one. Yeah, her ass was still crazy as fuck.

Nevada

"His tablet and charger are in the bag. Watch him with that charger because he wants to leave his shit plugged in all day. He runs through them like they're cheap. Don't forget he's allergic to latex—," I started but his grandmother cut me off.

"Girl, I didn't meet the boy last night. I know what he's allergic to." She rolled her eyes. "Get on out of here before you piss me off," she warned.

She was right. This wasn't Nita's first time watching Demari. But it'd been the first time this year because me and her triflin' son was beefing. She couldn't be one of those moms that minded her business. She wanted to involve herself in some shit her son only gave her half the tea to. So, I included her when I told him that I didn't want him around my son.

While his sisters and brothers called me a bitter baby mama, I kept my son within my blended, well-structured family. Jemari's family had too much going on. My seven-year-old son came home on a three-day suspension because he threatened to hang another classmate by his balls. He ain't heard that shit from nowhere but his daddy.

I tried to have a civilized conversation with him and instead, he wanted to show off in front of his new little girlfriend. So, I told his ass to take me to court for visitation. Of course, he didn't. I ain't have shit to be bitter about because I didn't need Jemari for shit. I made my own money, and my family supported me. Jamari didn't know shit about that because he was raised by and *with* wolves. A pack of fucking savages. And I wasn't scared of near one of them.

The only reason I decided to let Nita spend some time with him is because Damari said he missed her. His father had been locked up the last three months anyhow. I didn't see the harm in letting Damari spend the weekend with her. But if he came back home on that street shit, he'd be taking another break from his daddy's side of the family. And I didn't give a fuck who felt what about it. That's *my* son.

Leaving Nita's, I headed straight to the office building for this little show. A few weeks ago, I saw an ad for *Smoke with Me*. They were asking for girls to come out and participate. I ain't have shit else to do and I was looking for a new boo, so I signed up. I never imagined I would get picked to participate, but I did.

While sitting in the parking lot, a car whipped in next to me. Three girls sat there, fixing their hair and makeup. They must've been going to the same place I was. The girl in the passenger seat got out first and accidentally flashed me her coochie. She had on a skirt with no panties. The driver got out and twerked in the reflection of her window. The last girl's pinky toe repeatedly grazed the black concrete as she walked inside. My nose scrunched up on its own. If this was the type of women participating, I may have been in the wrong place.

My big sister was calling my phone like she could sense I needed encouragement. She had this weird way of being able to predict the future so clearly. If you asked her about it, she'd always shrug and say, "I can just see it playing out".

"Hello?" I answered.

"Where you at?" she asked.

"In the parking lot." I burst into laughter.

"Girl, if you don't take your scary ass in them people's office. If 'I don't need a man' was a person, it'd be you. We all need love, baby. We all deserve it," she encouraged.

"Then you should've come with me." I rolled my eyes as if she could see me.

"Don't start that shit," she warned.

Denver was in her first toxic relationship. The shit was changing her, and she couldn't see it. The gift she had of seeing the future never worked for her own life. She was blinded by love. But honestly, I think she was blinded by grief. A little over a year ago, she lost her best friend, Nae, to that fent. Denver hadn't been the same since. I truly think that she believes she is in love. In my opinion, the nigga just showed up when she was weak, vulnerable, and out of her fucking mind with heartbreak. She would have never chosen that nigga if she wasn't depressed when they'd met.

"Anyway, I want to go in here. I deserve a little fun. Somebody to lay up with when I don't have Damari. I just want to feel good. I just want to be loved on a little. But I've seen a few of the other girls, and it's giving desperate as fuck," I argued.

"You ain't going in there to date them. You don't even know if they his type of bitch or not. So, get your pretty, brown-skinned, long-haired ass out of that car and steal the show like you always do," she talked the shit that I hadn't been able to say to myself.

"Ard, I'm going," I told her.

"Call me when you finished. Love you!"

"Love you, too." I ended the call.

I entered the building just as two more girls were getting out of a car. I was only able to get a quick glance without looking like I was a fan or enemy. The elevator took so long that they ended up getting on with me. I stood against the back wall in my black and white dunks with thick black socks. My oversized tee, dangled over my biker shorts perfectly. I was simple compared to them.

One girl wore a sundress with strappy heels. The girl with her was almost as laid back as me with fatigues and a tee but a pair of opened toed heels that changed the entire fit up. She wore makeup but barely. She was almost as pretty as me. I had a feeling I was going to get in this room and be underdressed like a motherfucker.

"I don't know what you're nervous about," the dressed down one spoke. "Either way it goes, we about to have a bunch of niggas in our DMs. If he ain't the one, the one is right around the corner. If we have any luck, it's a nigga with some money."

They laughed as we stepped off the elevator. I loved to argue the niggas at the barbershop down about women. But the more these bitches talked on these podcasts and in these lives, the more I realized niggas were right. At least seventy- five percent of these bitches were looking to be taken care of. I'm a woman first. And I have a kid, so I understand wanting a man to provide some stability, but these women were the new bums.

Entering the room, the lighting was to die for. You wouldn't have to search for a good angle because the entire room was photo worthy. I didn't take selfies in public, though, so it was a missed opportunity. Once I was checked in, I went over to the little dispensary type set up they had for the weed.

There was a shelf with different packages of different strains. There were two dudes behind the counter, grabbing what we wanted. I waited for my turn, not needing to scan the different flavors. I already knew what I wanted. If they didn't have it, then this show was some Fu.

"Pick a strain, a blunt, and a lighter," the chubby dark-skinned dude said to me as I stepped up to the counter. On the opposite end, there was a nigga rolling blunts for the girls that couldn't roll.

"I want the Za, the honey berry backwoods, and the black-on-black Bic," I said, tossing my buss down over my shoulders.

"Ard." He reached for my backwoods but grabbed my weed from under the counter. I knew they had that shit. "See dude right there, and he gon' take care of you."

"I'm good," I told him.

I walked over to the table with the nigga rolling blunts and rolled my own shit. A few of the bitches snickered while whispering to each other. That shit ain't phase me. A bitch being shady was a bitch that ain't want no smoke for real. I hadn't spotted a bitch in here that I thought could whip my ass. I rolled my blunts and stuck them back in the package. What I didn't smoke here, I was taking home with me for later.

It was maybe fifteen minutes before the last three girls walked in. I'd been the only one to come alone. That's crazy. I always knew I was a standout bitch. And as expected, I was underdressed like a motherfucker. Once I was able to spark my blunt, I wouldn't give a fuck about that, or anything else for that matter.

They had us line up, side by side in a straight line. It was requested that we hold our blunts and lighters in our hand.

"Y'all ready to see who y'all smoking with?" Anton, the host, asked.

A few of the girls were over excitedly jumping up and down, a few twerking and being all around loud as fuck. One thing was for sure. You wouldn't be confused by what his type was by the end of this. If I wasn't his type, I wouldn't trip. I had some Za and a good ass lighter for my worries.

When the door opened and Ship appeared, I couldn't hide my smile. He had a fat ass blunt of something that had his eyes sitting low as a bitch. Whatever he had wasn't overpowering his cologne because when he walked in the room, you could smell it. I'd seen him on *Pretty Robots* with Poppie and thought he was fine as fuck. In that second, I was reminded of how extra Poppie was. I was not going to be Ship's type. *Damn.*

"Ard, ladies, you know what to do. Spark those blunts if you tryna smoke with Ship," Anton announced.

Ship looked around the room as six of us lit our blunts. The girl who got out of the car, flashing her pussy didn't light hers, and one of the three late bitches didn't light hers either.

"You wanna tell us your name and why you ain't light your blunt?" Anton asked.

"My name is—"

"Fuck I need to know your name for?" Ship cut her off.

Me and the two girls from the elevator burst into laughter. One of the other late girls put her blunt out.

"Because that's how the game works," the girl snapped on him. "My name is Candy, and I didn't light my blunt because I don't like light-skinned niggas," she said.

"Bitch, I'm light brown-skinned. You a fucking forty-year-old bitch walking 'round calling herself Candy." He twisted his lips up. "Fuck out of here."

"Nigga, who forty?" Candy asked.

"You might not be, but your face is." Ship waved her off.

I burst into laughter by myself this time, while the girl whose toes were hitting the ground and the last late bitch put their blunts out.

"Damn, what the fuck I do?" Ship tossed his arms up and me and fatigue burst out laughing.

"Let's do this in order," Anton interrupted. "You," he pointed to the other girl that never lit her blunt.

"Why didn't you light your blunt?" he asked her.

"Because we all know what he did to Street." The girl looked off.

"Yeah, I'm glad your ass didn't light your shit. I don't know what the fuck you talking about," he said with a straight face, denying her claims.

On *Pretty Robots*, Poppie's baby father was shot. The world assumed it was Ship, but there was never any proof of that.

"What about you?" he asked one of the late girls.

"He *is* sassy like Candy said he was." The girl shrugged. "He doing all that 'cause she gave her name. Like be fucking for real."

"Oh nah, you talk like me. I'm good on that anyway," Ship said.

Me and fatigue were laughing again. I had a feeling it was going to come down to me and her. And then eventually go to her because when he started asking his questions, I wasn't going to say what he wanted to hear.

"Ok, and you two?" The host looked to the girls that put their blunts out when Ship and Candy were going back and forth.

"He called her a bitch," one shrugged.

"Yeah, I didn't like that either," the other girl answered.

I rolled my eyes up in my head. He had them scared to give their names like they were supposed to. It was just me, the two girls from the elevator, and the driver of the three girls that arrived together. May the best bitch win.

Ship

"That went a little left," Anton said. "But Ship, now it's your turn. Who do you not want smoking with you?"

There were only four girls left. I had already pictured three of them sitting on my dick.

"I think all of y'all are attractive women. And I appreciate y'all coming out to do this stupid shit with a nigga," I said, trying to ease the blow.

"Aww, can I light my blunt again?" one of the girls who said they didn't like that I said the word bitch asked.

"Fuck no," I answered before Anton could. "I curse, baby. Bitch is my favorite word," I told her.

"Okay, Ship, let's focus. Who do you not want to smoke with?" he asked.

There were two shorties standing side by side like they came together, and one had on fatigues. There was a pretty ass bitch with Dunks on. And the last bitch was thick as fuck, but she had on too much fucking makeup. I couldn't picture her on my dick because I didn't know what the fuck she looked like for real.

"I'm sorry, sweetheart." I pointed to her.

"It's cool." She shrugged, putting her blunt out.

"Ard. Now that you're interested in them and they're interested in you, let's get to the questions."

"Do you have kids and how many?" I asked.

That was my first question because it was the most important. If there was a baby daddy, then she was more than likely tied to that nigga the way Peaches wanted to be tied to me. I ain't feel like dealing with a bitch who was just going to go back to the nigga she really loved later.

"I do," the girl in the Dunks answered. "Just one, and he's seven. I haven't slept with my baby father since my son was two." She laughed, and the shit made me laugh.

Before I got here, I said I was eliminating every bitch with a kid. But I was feeling her, so fuck that.

"Ard, now the ladies get to ask something. You." Anton pointed to the one standing next to the girl in the army fatigues.

"What's your real name?"

"Aw man," one of the niggas in the back said.

"Get her outta here," another egged me on.

"What I do?" she asked, confused.

"You asked him to say his government on a camera," Anton turned to her, biting his lip.

Everybody in the room knew she was gone. That was some simple shit. You either knew not to ask that or you didn't. I wasn't in the streets anymore, but that could change at any minute. And still, I wanted a street-smart bitch.

"Yeah, I'm sorry, sweetheart," I said.

"That's my bad." She put her blunt out. "I wasn't thinking."

I was left with the fatigue girl and the Dunks girl. Both of them were my speed. That baby daddy shit was still lingering in my head, though.

"Ship, what's your next question?" Anton asked.

"What do you do for work?"

I ain't want no begging ass bitch. By all means, I was a spoiler, but I didn't want to spoil no entitled motherfucker either. I got enough of that with Kong's ass. That's why I had to get my own whip. The nigga was getting beside himself with his corner store orders.

"I work at a daycare," the girl with the fatigues answered.

I liked that. She didn't have kids, but she knew how to deal with them. It was definitely a point in her favor. I nodded my head.

"I work at a barbershop. I cut hair," Dunks answered.

She was making it so hard to not eliminate her ass. What bitch worked at a barbershop? That meant she was around a new nigga every damn day. And whatever barbershop she worked at had regulars who had already been trying to make their way out of the friend zone. I ain't like that shit. I couldn't eliminate her just yet.

"Ard, ladies. It's your turn. You were next." Anton nodded his head to fatigues.

"My name is Amiya. What's your relationship with your mother like?" she asked me.

That was a good ass question. She was trying to get to know a nigga for real. My answer might turn her off and she'd eliminate herself. That'd make it easier for me.

"I don't have one," I said aloud.

"I'd take a nigga with no mother over a mama's boy any day," Amiya responded.

"Ard. Since both ladies are staying, Ship you have one last question. Make it count," Anton told me.

There was too much shit I wanted to know. One question

wasn't going to do it. But that's all I had. I wanted to ask something that Dunks couldn't fuck up, even if she tried. Something simple yet revealing still.

"Why you ain't put your blunt out yet?" I asked.

"Because," Amiya rushed to get her answer off first. "I've already pictured myself sitting on your dick," she answered.

I couldn't even be mad at it because I pictured the same shit. If we ain't have shit else in common, she was down to fuck. I wasn't looking for no relationship anyhow. I could appreciate the fact that she said that shit straight up with no shame. That said she ain't give a fuck about what nobody else thought of her. I liked that.

I looked over to Dunks, who was already on her second blunt. Before Anton could ask her for her answer, I did.

"Why you fucking with me?" I asked.

"I like your energy. You got this subtle confidence. You not trying to impress us. You not looking for us to impress you. The questions you asked make me think you're looking for something real. And while I would love to sit on that dick, too, I just wanna be up under you," Dunks answered. "My name is Nevada, by the way."

"Oh, shit. We got a competition now. What you gonna do, Ship?" Anton asked me.

The intimate space was intense. I was feeling both these bitches. They both looked good. Nevada did have the better answer, but that was just this time. Her earlier answers almost got her eliminated.

"I do know who I want," I confessed. "But I want to be fair. She didn't get to ask me anything yet. I want to hear her question first," I said, looking to Nevada.

Amiya gained some points for her question. She ain't ask

me no bullshit. It was only right to let Nevada get the same opportunity.

"Well, you heard the man. What's your question?" Anton asked Nevada.

"What time you picking me up tonight?" she asked.

The room went crazy. A nigga felt that shit. I couldn't even hide my smile. With that, she took the fucking cake.

"8 PM," I answered.

"I think we have a winner. Ship is going to smoke with Nevada!" Anton yelled into the mic.

I went to shake her hand, and we ended up dapping like we'd been old friends reuniting.

"What's your number?" She pulled her phone out.

I read my number off to her. She showed me my contact info, and it said Big Ship with a ship emoji, the anchor emoji, and the droplets of water.

"I'ma text you my address. My name better have some pretty emojis next to it when you pick me up," she said, walking backwards towards the door, biting her tongue.

I laughed her off with every intention of scrolling through all the emojis to find the perfect ones.

"As promised," Anton said, holding a rubber band stack. He put it in my hand. "Good show. I know the views gon' be up when this shit drops. And I think you got a good one," he said, dapping me up before walking off.

Leaving there, I headed to the crib. Kiss was on the game when I walked in the house. I ain't know if he was going to have his kids or not, but Savon wasn't running around, pretending to be a dinosaur, so I knew they weren't here. I loved my niece and nephew, but I was happy this motherfucker was kid free tonight.

It was a rare occurrence around this bitch.

"You find a bitch?" he asked, glancing away from the TV.

"Yeah, cute lil' bitch. I'ma take her out tonight. Hopefully bring her back to the crib and see what the pussy hitting for," I told him.

"That's what up," Kiss said. "I might call me a bitch up."

If Kiss called a bitch, he was going to her shit, putting some dick in her, and leaving immediately. That nigga was not playing about being off relationships. He was cool with him and Cambria being on again and off again. The one time he tried to move on, she was threatening him with moving back home. If he had someone and she didn't, it was a problem. But if she had someone, he never tripped.

At the end of the day, I think Kiss really wanted his family. But if he couldn't have her, he just wanted Cambria to be happy. Too bad she was an evil ass bitch. I wouldn't be the one to tell him that, though. The nigga ain't want you saying shit about his bitch. He minded his business when it came to my shit, too. He ain't give a fuck that I was still getting Rhea like she was mine. It was Kong still giving me shit about it.

After straightening up, Nevada sent me a text with her address. I jumped in the shower, tossed some fly shit on, and was out the door. It'd take twenty minutes to get to her place. I had thirty to spare.

When I arrived, I used the extra ten minutes to prettify her name in my phone. Once I found some shit, I texted her that I was outside. It took maybe ten minutes for her to walked out of the doors of her building. She slid in the car and didn't miss a beat.

"Lemme see my name in your phone." She leaned closer to my phone that was on the mount attached to the window.

“Damn.” I laughed. “How you doing and shit? You look nice, smell good, skin glowing and all that.”

“Thank you.” She laughed. “Now lemme see my name,” she ordered.

“Call my phone,” I told her, pulling out of the space.

She called and her name popped up with a chocolate candy bar. She scrunched her face up.

“I think I see where you going with this.” She smiled, nodding her head, ending the call.

“Ion really eat candy like that. But chocolate ain’t candy, it’s a confection.” Stopping at the red light, I glanced over at her.

“Ohhh,” she cheesed. “I like the big words and shit.” She got comfortable in her seat. “And you look nice as well. Smell better, too,” she flirted.

“Thank you, thank you.”

“So, where we going?”

“Wherever you want to go,” I told her.

“You supposed to plan the date.” She rolled her eyes, laughing.

“I did,” I argued, pulling off at the green light. “The plan was to take you wherever you want to go,” I told her. “Your outfit say you tryna do something chill. Comedy show maybe, bowling or some shit like that.” I glanced over to see her smiling. “You wanna go bowling?” I asked her.

“Yeah, I’m down.” She nodded her head. “That sounds fun. I damn sure ain’t want to do no typical shit.”

“I’m not a dinner and a movie type of guy. My nerves too bad to sit in a theater for that long. And I like my meals homemade,” I told her.

"What's your favorite home cooked meal?"

"I like red meat. I don't give a fuck which one. And I could eat mac and cheese and mashed potatoes every day. Only the homemade shit, though. You give me some quick whip shit, I might block your ass."

We laughed as I pulled up to the bowling alley. Nevada said she wanted to smoke first. She pulled out a blunt, took a few hales before passing it to me.

"What's your real name?"

"You the feds?" I asked her, taken aback.

"No, but how I'ma give you some pussy if I don't know your real name?" she asked, resting her head against the seat and looked at me innocently.

"Patrick Younger, Jr.," I told her.

Nevada

"You wanna bet something?" I asked Ship as we put the bowling shoes on.

"What you got for me?" he asked.

"When I win, we fuck at your place," I told him. I stood, walking over to the machine to input our names.

"What you mean *when*?" He joined me over at the machine. "I'm nice, baby."

"Bowl once a month nice?" I asked, locking our names in on the screen.

"Oh, you played a nigga," Ship laughed, nodding his head. "You got that. My crib is cool, though." He grabbed a ball. "We ain't gotta worry about baby daddies there." He raised his eyebrows before rolling his ball down the lane.

He knocked eight pins over, missing two. The second ball he threw knocked the last two pins over.

"We don't have to worry about them at my place either. Mine is locked up," I revealed. "And I already told you, I don't deal with him." I stood to take my turn.

"Bitches say a lot of shit," he said, sitting down and stretching his arms out across the bench.

"And niggas say even more shit," I reminded him as I tossed my ball down the lane. "Your turn," I told Ship, knowing that I had a strike.

"So, what's the story with that?" he asked, taking his turn.

"Exes on a first date?" I asked, watching him hit a strike. "That's a little cringe, don't you think?" I stood to take my turn.

"We got kids," he said. "That don't apply to us. I need to know who still around you. 'Cause my daughter be around *me*," he explained. "And to be real, a nigga wanna know if he can get comfortable. If this some shit where I see you when I see you, that's cool. I ain't tryna fall in love with you for you to belong to another nigga at the end of the day."

That shit distracted me, and my ball only hit two pins. Ship wasn't with the games. I felt that. I wasn't with that shit either. For me, the show was to find a little boo thang or whatever. Maybe this could be more than that.

I tossed my second ball. On the walk back, Ship pulled me into his lap. His shit was on soft, but I could still feel that print. I shouldn't have said shit about riding. My lil' coochie was going to need time to adjust to that motherfucker.

"We were together for a year," I started. "I was full on in love at twenty. Told my parents that I was moving out and moved in with him. We weren't in our place for a month before I got pregnant. I had a horrible pregnancy. Headaches, stomachaches, couldn't keep shit down. I guess it was too much for him because that's when the other bitches started popping up. Phone calls in the middle of the night, text messages first thing in the morning. He wouldn't come home for days at a time sometimes." I looked off.

This wasn't a story that I had to tell too many times. I kept a tight circle, and they were there in real time to see it happen. The niggas I entertained were just that. I couldn't take them seriously, so I didn't bother spilling my history with my baby father. It was embarrassing. Most of these niggas would take what you said and use it to manipulate you anyway. It was a waste of breath, feelings, a waste of a try.

Even the questions Ship asked in the dating show, made him stand out from the Baltimore City niggas I was used to. It helped that I saw Poppie cut him off for Street. I knew he was asking this because he didn't want to get played again. If we had a real chance at building something, why not go into it being real? No matter how embarrassing the shit was.

"I stayed because I thought things would get better once he saw his son. Like, he couldn't run from shit anymore. But he did. In fact, he got worse. My son's first birthday came, and we threw him a party. His father told me not to worry about anything because he was taking care of everything. And he did. Except the bitch who made my son's cake was a bitch he was fucking. So, I broke up with him. I did dibble and dabble until Demari was two. But I haven't touched that raggedy nigga since," I explained.

"Does he still want you?" Ship asked.

"He's long moved on," I said.

"That's not what I asked you."

"If I wanted him back, I think he'd go for it," I answered honestly, "but I don't want him," I assured Ship.

"I hear you. I'm sure my baby mother is off telling a nigga the same thing," Ship countered.

"Well, it might not be true for her, but it's true for me. So, you got a baby mother that still wants you, but you questioning me like you are one of Baltimore City's best in a uniform?" I laughed.

"My shit complicated. I'on want her ass, though. That's all that matters."

"How many kids y'all got together?" I asked him.

"Just one. My baby girl, Rhea. She's five years old." Ship smiled at the mention of his daughter.

"And what happened with you and her mother?" I asked since he was all in my business.

"We was together and now we not," he said, lifting me up and sitting me beside him.

He stood to take his turn. I felt a way. I spilled all my shit for him to give me two obvious sentences about him and his baby mother. This nigga was not playing fair. Red flag number one. I kept tally in my head.

I'd won our game. So, we knew when the night was over, we were going back to Ship's place. When we left the bowling alley, I asked if we could grab something to eat from America's Best Wings. We jumped in the car and headed in that direction.

"So, at the show, you said that you didn't have a mother. You adopted or something?" I asked.

"No," he laughed. "My mother a zombie. I'on claim her. I'on fuck with her."

"And your dad?" I asked.

"Never met him," Ship said, focusing on the road. "What about you? You know your peoples?" he asked.

"Yeah. I'm a daddy's girl, for real. He and my mama ain't been together in forever. But he's always been in my life. He's married, too. My stepmom is cool. Outside of my older sister, that also has a different mom, that's it. My mom got married when I was one, so my stepdad is like my father, too. I'm my mama's only child, but my stepdad has a son. He's in the military; he's hardly ever around, so I might as well be the only child still," I laughed. "I'm pretty close with my parents. We do holidays, vacations, allat together," I said. "Where do you usually spend the holidays?" I asked him.

"With my baby mother and my daughter," he said, plainly. "I don't mind changing that, though," he said when he noticed my expression changed.

"Good," I said as we pulled into the parking lot.

Ship led the way into the store. I told him what I wanted. While he placed our orders, I couldn't help but to recognize how regular this felt. It was like this was our normal. There was no awkward stage because it felt like I knew him already. We were getting the tough questions out of the way early. It felt like I was doing things the right way this time.

"For here or to go?" the cashier asked.

"To go," I spoke up.

"You tryna leave me already?" Ship came and stood behind me.

He wrapped his arms around my waist like I'd been his bitch forever. I see why he was worried about his little feelings. He was clingy than a motherfucker. I liked my niggas all over me, all the time, so we wouldn't have any issues in that department.

"No, I'm tryna get you home already." I lifted my head to whisper in his ear.

"I bet you thinking we can get in the bed," he whispered in my ear, "put a movie on while we eat. I'ma fuck the shit out of you, and then we gonna go to sleep," he said.

"Allat, except I'm going to fuck the shit out of you," I whispered back in his ear.

"I can't wait to see you try," he told me.

It wasn't long before the cashier called his name out. He grabbed our food and led the way to his car. We made a stop at the liquor store.

"You coming in?" he asked before getting out of the car.

"Mmhmm." I nodded, rushing out as Ship took the keys out

of the ignition.

He held the door open for me to walk in first. “What you feeling tonight?” he asked as we roamed the aisles of liquor. “You a Casamigos kind of girl?” He grabbed, lifting the bottle.

“Wrong sister,” I said. “All my sister drinks is tequila, straight, at that. But me, I like a good dark. What about this?” I grabbed the fifth of Disaronno.

“Hell yeah.” He took it from my hands. “That’s my shit.”

“Bet.” I followed him to the register.

We checked out, catching looks from other couples in the store like they wanted to join us for the night. I wouldn’t let a bitch eat my pussy if her tongue came with a vibrator. I wasn’t into girls at all.

“So, what kind of drunk are you?” Ship asked as he held the door open for me to leave. “Am I fitna be babysitting all night?”

“No.” I laughed. “I’m a horny drunk. I just wanna fuck and sleep. Wake up and do it again. That’s too much for you?” I asked, getting into the car.

“Nah, that’s just my speed,” he said as we pulled off.

“How do you feel about threesomes?” I asked, still thinking about all the people that were looking at us in the store.

“You gotta friend or something?” he asked.

“Nah, that’s not my thing. I like toys and shit, though,” I told him honestly.

“What that’s gon’ do for me? That’s for you and your solo shit,” he shot back.

“Oh, this is going to be fun. Next time we link, we can link at my place. I can show you some shit. Turn you out a little bit.”

“Turn me out?” He scrunched his face up. “I don’t like the

sound of that," he shook his head.

"Ain't that what niggas say to good girls and shit?" I shot back.

"Yeah, but when you say turn a nigga out, that sound like some gay shit. Say turn a nigga up or something. I don't know, but don't say that no more."

We laughed as he parked in front of what I assumed to be his house. We got out the car with him carrying the food and me carrying the bottle.

"I don't know if I told you, but my brother stay here," he warned me as he unlocked the door. "And not on no bum shit. We go fifty/fifty on this motherfucker."

"You didn't, but that's cool," I said as we walked in. "Just keep it down. Don't be screaming and shit," I joked.

"Stop playing with me." Ship laughed as we stepped into the crib.

"What's up?" Ship and his homeboy dapped one another up. "Kiss, this is Nevada. Nevada, this is my brother, Kiss."

"Nice to meet you." I extended my hand for dap.

"You, too." He dapped me up.

He only gave me a glance. I don't even think it was more than a second. Weird ass nigga.

I know I should've been wanting a nigga to have his own shit. And I did, but this confirmed that he ain't have no bitch in his life for real. Not nothing heavy with nobody. If he did, the bitch ain't care about him none. The economy was fucked up, so it made sense that people needed roommates. I could see this shit with Ship lasting. I hoped Kiss could afford this rent by himself.

Ship

We smashed that food watching the new Tyler Perry movie. That shit was wild. I ain't really like the shit, but she loved it. We didn't have the same taste in movies. A nigga didn't mind it, though. Shit was starting to feel too good to be true. I ain't like that feeling. I just wanted to coast in some good shit. When it came tumbling down on me, I knew it would tumble away even faster.

"What's up with ya homeboy? What's wrong with him?" Nevada asked me.

"My brother, and what you mean?"

I liked this. She could keep the issues coming. I could move through that shit. A nigga could get comfortable.

"He ain't even look at me," she said. "What, he got anxiety or something?"

"PTSD, like the rest of the city. What you want him looking at you for?" I asked.

"I don't, but when you're meeting someone for the first time, the normal thing to do is to make eye contact."

"Stop playing on my brother top. He just don't be fucking with the bitches we bring around. You sis or you nothing. And he don't know if you gon' be in here next week, so you nothing to him right now. If he saw you on the street, he would've looked at you. Nigga just got respect. Something you ain't used to, working in a barbershop prolly," I shot back.

"You don't like that I work in a barbershop? Typical nigga," she said.

"Typical bitch, tryna be up in niggas' faces and shit," I said.

"You good?" she asked, face scrunched up like she wanted to do something to me.

"Is you good? What, you want to fight?" I laughed.

"I do." She grabbed one of my pillows and swung it in my face.

I got off the bed, grabbed her by her leg as she tried to kick herself free. I was in between her legs, taking them hits she was throwing. I scooped her little ass up and tossed her on the bed. She gave up, stretching her arms out on the bed, laughing.

"My bad. I didn't mean no disrespect to your bother," she said, looking at me seriously. "Did you shoot Street?" she asked.

"Why you asking me incriminating shit?" I asked.

"Because I want to know. If I'm letting you put your dick in me, I should be able to ask whatever I want. I have a right to know what I'm getting myself into."

"You have a right to know what I'm out here doing from this point on. Anything I did before you ain't ya business," I told her flat out.

"It's not my business, but I want to know who I'm dealing with. There's not a bone in my body that wants to be with my baby father. The thought of him touching me makes my skin crawl. But at the end of the day, he is still my son's father. Demari needs him. I ain't going to hold you, though. My baby father gonna talk his shit. He ain't never seen me taking another nigga seriously before. If you gon' try to take his head off for that, then we gotta end this right here. No matter how good it feels already," she said, staring at the ceiling.

"Come here." I reached for her.

Nevada crawled into my lap. That fat ass was arched perfectly, and I couldn't wait to bend her ass over.

"I didn't shoot Street," I answered her honestly.

"Did Kiss do it?" she asked.

"You doing too much." I laughed a little.

She was wrong again. Kong shot Street. Everybody just thought it was me 'cause Street was talking shit to me. I had my gun out to lay that nigga the fuck down, but Kong was impatient. He shot his shit before I ever let mine off.

"I ain't gon' kill your baby father. But if he gets to talking that rowdy, rowdy shit, I can't say someone else won't. So, when that nigga finds out what you got going on with me. Nah." I shook my head. "Before he finds out, you need to tell him to mind his motherfucking manners," I told her softly before kissing her lips. "I don't give a fuck what shit he talks to you about me. That nigga need to keep his feelings off the internet, though."

"When things get serious, I'll talk to him." She nodded her head. "He's supposed to be home soon."

"You not understanding. The second I hit that shit, it's mine," I told her. "You need to tell that nigga whatever you need to tell him, now."

I was done with bitches going back to the nigga they left before they met me. The grass was greener with me. I knew it, and they knew it. Still, they wanted to work it out and try to turn that brown ass, dry ass grass they had, green. Them niggas would never be me.

"Ok." She nodded her head with a smile. "I'll talk to him the next time he calls Demari."

"And I meant what the fuck I said about that barbershop. You like that attention. I ain't tryna hear it," I told her.

"I do," she said honestly. "It's nice to hear how good you look. How good you smell. How if you were his, you'd never have to work again. Even if it's all lies. It's nice to hear," she whispered, looking off.

"So, if I tell you that shit every day, then what?"

I held her chin and made her face me. Women could curse you the fuck out and look you dead in your eye like a fucking demon. But when it came time to turn that muscle man shit off, they couldn't make eye contact for shit. I liked to read a motherfucker's eyes when they talked to me.

"I don't know, but you haven't said it today yet." I looked down at my watch. "And it's already 12:02 am."

"You look good. And you smell good," I told her.

"You forgot one," Nevada laughed.

"You got to work over here, baby." I laughed with her.

"Then replace it with something else," she whined.

"Ard. You look good, you smell good, and I wish I met you sooner."

Nevada leaned forward, kissing me rough as fuck. She was sucking my tongue like a vacuum. I couldn't wait to see what she was going to do with the dick. Nevada pulled her shirt over her head. Her titties bounced in my face as she gyrated her hips onto my lap. She was acting like she was in heat. The shit had me rock hard.

She climbed off of me and tooted that ass up in the air on my side. She pulled my dick from my boxers and sucked me like I was her favorite flavored lollipop. I gripped Nevada's hair, humping into her mouth. She gagged on my shit. There was so much spit on my dick, it was dripping down to my thighs.

"Chill, chill, chill. You fitna make me nut." I tried to get away from her ass. I had to literally push her head away to get her to let me loose. "Gah damn." I ran my hands down my face. "Take them motherfucking shorts off." I smacked her ass.

I stood from the bed, pulling my shirt over my head. I came out of my shorts then my boxers. Nevada bent over on all fours, spreading her cheeks apart. Damn, this bitch was something else. I know she wanted the dick, but I had to taste her. I sucked on her clit like the shell of a sunflower seed. Nevada moaned as she humped against my face.

I couldn't take that shit no more. I slid into her slowly. That pussy was tight. I worked her until that motherfucker was opening up for me. Nevada started creaming around my dick, and that was all she wrote. I came in her with hard thrusts, trying to hit her stomach.

"What the fuck," she said, stretching out on the bed.

"Let me get you a rag," I said, clearing my throat.

In the bathroom, getting Nevada a warm rag, I had post nut clarity. The fuck was a nigga doing? Out here being fucking reckless. I wrung the rag out and carried it in the room to Nevada.

"Thank you." She took the rag from my hand, cleaning herself.

"You're welcome."

"We gotta stop and get a Plan B in the morning," she said, passing me the rag back. "So, you better make that round two count."

Nevada crawled to her spot in my bed, got under the covers, and adjusted the pillow until she was comfortable. A nigga didn't even have to ask her about the Plan B. She was already on it.

"Get in the bed," she whined.

"I'm coming," I told her.

I wiped my dick clean in the bathroom before going back in the room. I climbed into the bed. Nevada immediately moved her body until her ass was against my dick. Then my phone rang.

Nevada popped her head up, eyeing me up and down. Peaches was calling me. It was damn near two in the morning. It could be something with Rhea, so I had to answer.

"Hello?" I cleared my throat.

"You must have had a good date because you didn't even call Rhea to say good night," she said as if she was unbothered.

The fact that she was calling at all said that she was in her chest about me moving on.

"You couldn't have called me 'bout that in the morning?" I asked.

"You go out on one date, and now I got hours of operation and shit? What the fuck ever, Ship."

Peaches ended the call. Nevada finally stopped staring at me and laid her big head ass down. She ain't waste no time being in my business.

"Was that your baby mother?" she asked.

"Yeah," I answered honestly.

"Seemed like the perfect time to tell her about me. You know?" she said.

I was going to tell Peaches that I was kicking it with somebody. Two in the morning wasn't the time to do that. She was already calling to fish anyway. Her ass knew I wasn't up this time of night. I might've moved too fast with Nevada. The one time I actually had a bitch that wasn't in love with another nigga, I was about to fuck it up.

Nevada

"Bitch!" My sister grabbed her phone from her tripod and put her face in the camera as I swallowed my pill. "Is that a motherfucking Plan B?" Her eyes went wide.

"Yes, and cut the dramatics. You always saying that Demari is enough, so..." I shrugged.

"I was wondering why your ass ain't call me after you left that damn show. I told you to find love, not a fuck. Shit. You could've found that at the corner store." She rolled her eyes at me.

"Who says I didn't find love?" I argued.

"The water that helped push that Plan B down your throat," Denver said as she placed her phone back on the tripod.

"Well, it will be soon. In fact, the next time Jemari calls, I'm going to let him know I'm seeing someone." I shrugged at the camera.

"And you'd be a dummy. You don't even know that nigga. Ain't no point in getting Jemari's loose screwed ass all upset."

"It was Ship from *Pretty Robots*." I raised my eyebrows.

"Bitch, I know you lying!" Denver was finally showing some excitement for me.

"Nope. And the nigga on me bad." I cheesed with my tongue out.

"Well, shit, you better tell Jemari while he still locked up and shit. It'll give him some time to calm down because we saw what happens when a nigga get to talking to Ship crazy." Denver laughed.

"Shut all that loud ass cackling up. Damn. It's nine in the fucking morning," her boyfriend said in the background.

"Bitch, who you talking to?" Denver snapped on Vince. "You don't pay for shit around this motherfucker. You want some peace and quiet, go to your mama house so I can get some, too. The fuck!"

"Girl, go ahead. I'm pulling up at Nita's house anyway. I'll call you later," I told her.

"Why you ain't say that shit before I went off on him? Now I look dumb. Bye, bitch."

Denver hung up on me as I laughed. I loved my sister. We were so close, it was like we grew up in the house together. In reality, we only saw each other on weekends until we were old enough to visit one another on our own. She'd stay at my house sometimes. I'd stay at hers. My mama treated Denver like she was her own. Denver's mom did the same. Our family was definitely blended, but it wasn't broken.

I knocked on Nita's door with the sun beaming on my back. A bitch wasn't even upset about it today. We had a cold ass winter, and spring showed up doing its big one.

"Good morning, mommy!" Damari opened the front door.

"Good morning, son."

He rushed me for a hug. I rubbed his back and placed a few kisses to his forehead. My baby was too big for me to be picking him up like I used to. He was going to be as tall and stocky as his daddy. He looked just like his ass, too. My mama said it was because I hated Jamari when I was pregnant. I thought it was genes, but old people said any fucking thing.

When I looked at my son, all I could see was his father. It didn't get under my skin. It didn't frustrate me. Mostly, it made me want to love him the way Jamari should have been loved as a child. Maybe he wouldn't be such a triflin' nigga if somebody took care of him properly. The sad reality was no matter how much I loved on Damari, it would never transfer to Jamari. It wouldn't make him better.

"Mommy, I want some IHOP."

"You ain't eat?" I asked him.

"Yeah, he ate," Nita snapped. "You think I ain't feed my grandbaby? I fed your ass when you were pregnant with him. Let's not act brand new. The boy just greedy. And spoiled. You better get that up out of him now."

"Spoiled is for misbehaved kids. Damari is a good kid. I'm going to give him everything he asks for," I assured her.

"Yeah, that'll raise him to be a man," she mumbled.

"Get your stuff," I told Damari.

Me and Nita were about to get into it. I could feel it in my bones. She was commenting on my parenting, and that's where we always fell out. She couldn't tell me shit about being a good mom when her children were individually fucked up in different ways. If she said something that made sense, I'd be open to listening. Telling me that my seven-year-old should be told no for the sake of building his character was bullshit. I wasn't subscribing to that black family tradition. I wasn't putting him out at eighteen either.

"There you go, trying to run out of here 'cause you don't like what I'm saying," Nita said.

"I'm trying to get out of here, 'cause you not going to like what I'm saying once I get to saying it."

Damari reappeared with his black backpack in his hands.

"Come on." My hand on my head directed him to the door. "Say bye to your grandmother."

"Bye, Nana," he said, before stepping out of the door.

If I had any luck, he wouldn't want to see her for a while. She was on his time. If he didn't mention her, I wouldn't either.

"Did you have fun?" I asked him in the car.

"Yeah. Auntie Anna got me some new shoes. She said I got to keep them at Nana's, though. And Uncle Tony got me a PS5, but he said that it had to stay at Nana's, too. And Nana made me some banana pudding. It was so, so, so, good, mommy."

"That's good. I'm glad you had fun," I said.

He couldn't see it, but I was pissed. I wasn't the mom who told my son that he couldn't take his things with him when he visited with his other side of the family. If it was his, then it was his to do what he wanted with, within reason of course. Because at the end of the day, if they didn't send it back, I was going to get it.

I never kept anything they sent home with him to spite them. Happy people weren't petty. But I was human and triggered by pettiness. If they wanted to play those games, I'd play them bigger and better.

I'd block their numbers on his phone, forget to invite them to birthday parties, plan something fun for him whenever he asked about seeing them so that he was no longer thinking about it. I didn't do shit like that because I knew it would hurt Demari more than them. But damn, if they weren't tempting me.

"Yes!" Damari screamed when we pulled into the IHOP parking lot.

"What you getting?" I laughed as we got out of the car.

"Ooh, I want them pancakes with the blueberries, mad

bacon and some eggs, too," he said excitedly.

Damari grabbed the door and held it open for me. This was why I always had IHOP money, McDonald's money, and whatever he wanted money.

"Thank you, Mari."

"You welcome, mommy."

We were seated in a booth and placed our orders as soon as the waitress asked what we'd like to drink. My phone dinged as we waited.

BIG Ship: I miss you

This is what the talking stage was made of. That nonchalant shit never made my pussy wet. I wanted a nigga who toted guns, cursed a lot, but turned into a teddy bear for me.

Me: I miss you, too

Jemari used to be just like that. Except he was heavy in the streets. He wasn't toting guns as a just in case. He was putting them bitches to work. But when it came to me, he was as soft as a Cashmere sweater. That's what made me fall for him. It helped me love him longer than I should have. Well, helped me stay because I never stopped loving him. He's my son's father. My son is my biggest blessing, my most proud moment, and the very air that I breathe. Couldn't hate the nigga who gave him to me.

But I also understood that he could not be the man that I needed. Until crossing paths with Ship, I didn't think any nigga could be what I wanted. It was only a night, but last night felt like forever. Like we'd done this shit a million times already. I'd be playing myself to not take it as seriously as it appeared Ship was. Although, he had the perfect opportunity to tell his baby mother about me and opted out.

Ship needed me to tell Jemari about us. He needed me to leave my job. Those weren't his words, but I could already tell it would be a constant argument in our relationship when we got there. And I needed him to be all in to do that. I couldn't risk jumping out there just for Ship to let me fall. I was done giving more than I was getting. Ship had to be willing to give up everything that came against us, if he wanted that from me.

"Mari, I have a question," I asked him as he dropped a few blueberries into his mouth.

"What's up?"

"How would you feel if mommy had a boyfriend?"

I studied his face as he thought about it. At seven, Mari was smart as shit, but there were still feelings that he didn't understand enough to put into words. And there were words that he hadn't come across yet to explain what he was feeling.

"Like how Pop be having girlfriends?" He scrunched his face up like something stank.

"No. Daddy changes girlfriends like he changes his underwear. I mean like Grandma and Pop Pop," I offered a better example.

"They married," he argued.

"Yes." I nodded. "But before they were married, they were engaged to be married. That's when Pop Pop gave Grandma a ring and asked her to marry him. And before that, they were boyfriend and girlfriend," I gave a detailed explanation.

"He gon' take me fishing and stuff? I wanna get better at basketball so I can be rich and buy you a house. He can buy me sneakers?" He raised his eyebrows. "That's what Gabriel's stepdad does for him. He got two fathers."

"I can take you fishing and stuff, buy you sneakers," I mocked him, waving my head like a bobble head collector's item. "And I play basketball with you all the time."

"Yeah, but you're a girl. Nobody else's mama is on the court with them."

I never thought about it before, but he was right. I was the only mom out there on the court. And to be honest, it was only because I couldn't imagine sending him off and not having eyes on him. A bitch couldn't make a basket if Ship's tall ass held me up to the rim. I was just out there playing with him so he wouldn't be getting looked over or tossed around by the older boys out there.

Me: You know how to play basketball?

I sent Ship a text. If he didn't know, then I was going to have to learn. My baby wasn't out there trying to have a good time. He was trying to buy me a house.

"So, does that mean you are ok with mommy having a boyfriend?" I asked for clarity.

"Yeah, that's cool." He nodded, stuffing his extra strips of bacon in his mouth.

BIG Ship: Yeah, but I'm better at football. Why? You tryna play me for my heart?

I burst into laughter reading his text.

"I've asked you before what you wanted to be when you grew up. It changes every time I ask. Is a basketball player your final decision?" I asked Mari.

"Mmhmm," he nodded. "I want to be a basketball player."

That's all I needed to hear to go get everything he needed. I was already on my phone, googling local leagues I could get him into come summertime. If he didn't make it to the league, it wouldn't be because the opportunity wasn't in front of him. He could forever get the world from me.

"Well," I started cleaning up our mess, "when you become

a rich and famous basketball player, you won't have to buy mommy a house. I'll already have one. You don't ever have to hand money to me. I'm leaving you the world," I assured him.

I learned that from my own parents. It was my belief that it worked like that in all families. But once Denver and I were old enough to work, I got a dose of reality through her. She and her mom borrowed money back and forth. Denver had to pay bills at home. I never had to pay for anything until I turned eighteen and decided that I wasn't going to college. When my relationship with Jamari failed, my parents gave me every dime I paid from eighteen to twenty for a security deposit and first month's rent in the apartment I still live in now. They wanted to see me win. I wanted to see Demari be the biggest.

Ship

"You's a fucking simp," Kong spat at the break room table.

We weren't allowed to leave the building for lunch because we got paid breaks. So, we got shit out the vending machine every day. Basically, giving them back the money they paid us.

"Nigga, fuck you," I said back.

"You known this bitch for one day." He held his finger up for emphasis. "And you talking about telling Peaches about her." He scrunched his face up, stretching his arms up and out before letting them fall to his sides.

"Yeah, I gotta agree with Kong on this one, bro," Kiss chimed in. "That shit risky. You know how these bitches be with their kids. The first thing out her mouth going to be that she don't want that bitch around Rhea. And I know you hate hearing this shit but at the end of the day, Rhea ain't yours. Peaches can snatch her out your life whenever she feels like it."

He was right. I didn't want to hear that shit. A nigga ain't need no reminders that Rhea wasn't mine. And I understood his point, but Peaches needed a nigga. Wasn't nobody helping her, let alone her and a kid. I was the most decent nigga she ever fucked with. She'd fall in line because she didn't have a choice.

"On second thought," Kong licked his fingers. "Go head and tell Peaches about this new bitch. I think it's a *great* idea."

"Nigga." Kiss shook his head, laughing. "You don't know when to quit."

"Say what y'all want. I'm looking out for my brother. Peaches don't give a fuck about you, boy. When she finds her another nigga, she snatching Rhea from you like she was never yours. Because she wasn't. And that shit going to hurt ten times worse because you not going to see that shit coming. I don't know why you keep putting all this faith in that bird ass bitch. You couldn't trust her when y'all were together. You damn sure can't trust her ass now that y'all ain't. I'm just trying to prepare you." Kong shrugged.

"Well, I done already put my foot in my mouth with Nevada, so I gotta stand on it now," I told them as we cleared the table to go back to work.

"Stupid nigga," Kong said, shaking his head.

"I know, I know, what's going on with y'all niggas and y'all's bitches?" I asked, taking myself out of the hot seat.

"I ain't got no bitch," Kiss responded.

Kong and I both twisted our lips up at this nigga. Kiss was full of shit. He and Cambria could claim they was broken up, but they still moved like a fucking family unit, even in two different houses.

"I don't know what the fuck y'all looking at me like that for. We co-parenting. That's what good co-parenting looks like. I don't give a fuck what she doing. And she don't give a fuck what I'm doing."

"She don't give a fuck or she don't know?" I laughed.

"She don't need to know," Kiss retorted. "We ain't together and we ain't getting back together. I'm done with that relationship shit. I'm ok with just fucking a bitch when a nigga wants a nut. Then, going back to my kids because I don't give a fuck about shit else."

That part I could believe. Kiss ain't even come outside like that no more. Here and then we spent all night in the casino, but that was to make money for his kids. Everything revolved around them. I wanted to tell that nigga he deserved to be happy too, but he ain't believe that shit. We've done some fucked up shit, but we changed. All of us. Even Mont before he passed. Kiss was the only one who hadn't swiped any of that shit to the back of his head.

Back at my workstation, Rhea FaceTime me. I went and got her a phone one day when Peaches was playing games with answering my calls. Her house, her rules, but if she tried to take Rhea's phone, she'd have to deal with her tantrums all day long. It was a win-win for me.

"Hey, daddy." Rhea whispered when she saw my face.

"Why you calling me during nap time?" I twisted my lips up at her. "Go to sleep," I told her.

"I just wanted to say I love you." She blew me a kiss. "Bye, daddy."

The phone hung up, and a nigga was in the middle of his shift getting teary eyed. I loved Rhea more than anything in the world. Still, I think she loved me more than her little, tiny heart would allow. If I stepped away, it would hurt her just as much. It was too late for that. She knew me as her father. And when a nigga was dead and gone, she was going to remember me as her father. She wasn't going to have random thoughts of the first nigga to break her heart. Fuck that.

The shit was simple for me. I was going to tell Peaches that I was stepping into something serious with Nevada. She was going to act like a mature adult, and then we'd all live happily ever after. Kong and Kiss put that negative shit in my head, and I was reconsidering the risk I was taking.

I sat my phone on the shelf and FaceTime Nevada. She answered on the first ring with a smile on her face.

"What's up?" I smiled back.

"Nothing, sitting here and waiting on my next client," she said. "How's work?" she asked, resting her head against her wrist.

"It's cool. Moving slower than a motherfucker, though. What we doing this weekend?" I asked her.

"Whatever you want to do," she answered.

"You sure you wanna roll with that?" I raised my eyebrows.

"I mean, last weekend we did what I wanted. It's only fair, right?" She shrugged. "But it's going down at my house this time. And I'm pulling the toys out," she whispered into the screen.

"Ard, man. Go head back to work." I shook my head.

"My client just walked in anyway. I'll hit you later." Nevada blew a kiss into the phone before hanging up.

Again, I was pulled in the opposite direction. It was too risky *not* to tell Peaches about Nevada. We were literally only a few days in, but the shit felt real. We just naturally fell into place. I'd be a dumb ass not to see where it goes all because Peaches might get upset.

Me: I'm coming by to talk when I get off

I sent Peaches a text. In my head, I planned a million ways to start the conversation. I coached myself through imaginary scenarios of how I would break the news to her. A nigga was going to be soft spoken but direct. Straight to the point, but not short with her. I could do this shit.

Lying ass bitch: If I'm free. I'll let you know. You don't decide shit about what the fuck I got going on.

Reading her message made me look up to the ceiling. Eyes closed, I took a deep breath, shaking my phone in my hand. You need the patience of a dead man to deal with this bitch. She did have a point, though. Especially when I was going over there to tell her some shit she didn't want to hear. Being soft spoken couldn't start once I was there. It was a part of the buildup, so I took the L on that and texted her back.

Me: You right, that's my fault. I wanted to run something by you. If you free later, let me know.

Lying ass bitch: Yeah, that's cool. Hit me when you on your way.

She responded immediately and calmly. Maybe I was the problem. Whatever the case, I needed to get my speech together. I didn't want to lose Rhea or Nevada. To keep them both, I had to keep the lying ass bitch happy.

"Cambria here." Kiss was shutting his locker as me and Kong were walking up. "I catch you in the house," Kiss said to me.

"Ard." Me and Kong dapped him up and he walked off.

"That nigga a simp, too," Kong said as we opened our lockers up.

"That nigga a simp one!" I barked in Kong's face. "I'm not a simp one, two, or three, bitch." I slammed my locker shut. "That nigga is a simp, though."

Cambria ran Kiss's life. He was so scared of stepping out of line and her moving her ass back to her hometown. He had his moments when he went off. But there were more moments of her doing whatever she wanted and him sitting back, taking it. That's why that nigga was so against relationships and love or anything that looked like them.

Because at the end of the day, Cambria wasn't going to let his ass move on ever. She could date here and date there, but bro couldn't do shit. I couldn't wait for that nigga to open his eyes. It's real love out this motherfucker, not love of convenience or responsibility. He was never going to know that if he kept allowing Cambria to dangle the possibility of them getting back together over his head. He claimed he wanted to be single; that nigga wanted his baby mother.

Parting ways with Kong, I headed home to shower. I shot Peaches a quick text that I was on my way before I left out the house. So, why she wasn't home when I got there was pissing me off. I remained calm and called her to find out where she was.

"Hello?" she answered.

"I thought you said it was cool to come by and talk. Where you at?" I asked her.

"I'm in the house," she said.

"Where your car at?" I asked, getting out of the car. I did a quick look around the complex, and her shit wasn't out here.

"My little boo got it. He went to do my little bit of grocery shopping while we talked," she explained.

That shit almost made me walk back to my car. I ain't give her the car for her to be letting some broke ass, bum ass nigga drive my shit like it was his. A bitch with a whole kid ain't have no business fucking with a nigga that ain't have his own fucking whip. And if she chose to hand her pussy over to the bum, she shouldn't be letting that nigga drive the car I bought her. And why was the nigga buying groceries like he lived there?

"What's up?" Peaches asked as I walked in the house.

I heard the three beeps through my Air Pod, signifying that Peaches ended our call.

"Hi, daddy!" Rhea stretched her arms out to me.

She was on the floor in between Peaches's legs getting her hair braided. Peaches had on some bedtime shorts that looked like strings against her big ass thighs. I leaned down to kiss

Rhea, leaving her where she was, despite wanting to scoop her up and squeeze her. Peaches was always on a nigga back about distracting Rhea. We had enough shit to talk about.

"What you wanted to holla at me about?" Peaches asked me.

"That n-word living here?" I asked like that was a part of the conversation I came over to have.

"What n-word?" Rhea asked.

"Nickels," I answered, never taking my focus off of Peaches.

"Nah, he's stopped by the last two days, though. Like I said, he's doing me a favor. He don't just be driving my shit around all willy nilly and shit like you used to do to go see bitches," she reminded me of some of the shit I put her through. "I didn't think it was a big deal because you said we were over." She shrugged.

"But what that got to do with having some stranger a-word, n-word up in here around my daughter and s-word?" I asked her.

"That's a lot of words, daddy," Rhea remarked, unable to keep up.

"Daddy, sorry. I'll go slower next time," I assured her.

"He's not a stranger," Peaches said, avoiding eye contact.

Like, all of a sudden, she couldn't do a fucking braid without staring at it like it needed a babysitter. I spent half my shit, all my time in the shower and the ride over here, telling myself to be respectful. Warning myself not to get loud with the bitch. I wanted to knock this bitch head between the washer and dryer. The fuck she mean this nigga wasn't a stranger? If she said what I thought she was going to say, a nigga was going to need bail money like a motherfucker.

“Who is he?” I asked her.

She finally looked at me and mouthed the words “Rhea’s daddy.” Before I could think about my actions, I swiped a photo from the nightstand, separating the sectional from the recliner.

“The fuck you say?” I stood from my chair.

“Ship, relax,” Peaches stood, moving away from me.

“Nah, I ain’t hear that shit. Say that shit again.” I moved closer to her, knocking every movable item from its place. Pictures shattered, the millions of colorful beads scattered across the carpet.

“Her daddy,” Peaches whispered.

I had her cornered behind the front door. She slid down the door, tears coming down her face.

“So, you knew who this nigga was the whole time!” I barked on her. “You knew where to find him and allat?!”

“No!” she yelled, covering her head as if I ever put my hands on her stupid ass.” We ran into each other,” she explained. “What you wanted me to do, Ship?” she asked. “I’m not doing that single mother shit if I don’t have to! My baby needs her father!”

“She already got a fucking father!” I yelled in Peaches’s face. “Bitch, move!” She hurried to get away from the door. I snatched the door open like a teenage girl with an attitude because she couldn’t go to the mall. I don’t give a fuck how sassy the shit was. A nigga was fucked up. “Goofy ass bitch,” I mumbled, storming out of the house.

When I made it to the car, I realized that Rhea didn’t exist in that moment. I didn’t know where she was. I didn’t see her. I didn’t hear her. I just wanted to beat Peaches’s ass. Against my desire to pull away, I stormed back inside the house. Rhea was crying while Peaches was pressing buttons on her phone. I didn’t know who she was calling, and I didn’t give a fuck either.

I scooped Rhea up in my arms. “Daddy, sorry, baby.” I kissed her forehead. I rested my head against hers, bouncing her up and down until she stopped crying. When she sat up in my face and wiped her eyes free of tears, I told her, “Daddy love you, okay? No matter what anybody says, daddy loves you more than anything in this world, ok?”

Rhea nodded her head. “Why you so angry, daddy?”

“Daddy gotta go,” I ignored her question. “Tell me you love me, too.”

“I love you, too. Can I go with you?” she asked.

“Not tonight, baby. Daddy gotta work in the morning.” I sat her on the couch.

I planted a few more kisses to her forehead and walked out of the apartment. I thought to wait in my car for the bitch ass nigga to pull up. But it wasn’t his fault that Peaches was a trifling bitch. I ain’t have no beef with that nigga.

Peaches

"How you doing?" a fine ass light brown skinned nigga asked me.

"I'm good, how you?" I asked, sliding his groceries across the scanner and into the white plastic bags.

I'd been working at the grocery store for a few months. Overtime had me in here seven days a week. He'd never been in here before. He looked like a Baltimore nigga, dressed like a Baltimore nigga, and he talked like one, too. Maybe he was just moving to the East Side.

"A nigga straight, for real," he said.

"Not with all these packs of noodles you buying," I laughed. "You don't know how to cook?" I asked him.

"Nah, you tryna cook for me?" He licked his lips.

Hell yeah I was. I'd wash his draws and suck him every day and twice on Sundays. The nigga I was fucking with just got sent off to Job Corps by his daddy. I ain't have no boo. His ass was right on time. I grabbed my phone from the register and handed it to him.

"Put your number in my phone," I told him.

"I just got released today. I ain't even grab a phone yet," he told me. "Hold up." He walked off to the entrance of the store and grabbed a sales paper. He ripped a piece off and passed it to me. "Put your number on there."

I did him one better. I wrote my name, number, and my

address. He said his name was Ship as he grabbed his bags to leave the store.

He didn't hesitate to use it either. He hit my phone around ten that night, saying that he was outside. I'd just gotten out of the shower and rushed downstairs in my jammies.

"What's up?" I walked up on him and wrapped my arms around his neck.

"You live alone? I'm tryna get this nut up off me," he said.

"No, but my mama prolly in there fucking, too. Come on."

My mom and I were more like homegirls than parent and child. And if one of us was the parent, it was me. All my mother cared about was being laid up under some nigga. Broke, balding, or some dirty Air Forces, she didn't give a fuck. She couldn't breathe without a man. I worked because I had to. She damn sure wasn't going to make sure the lights didn't get cut off. When Ship and I walked past her bedroom, we could hear the grunts of a nigga probably getting her best work. She was trying to lock in a new man because the last one left her ass.

In my bedroom, we could hear her headboard knocking against the wall. I was too used to it to be disgusted. But I could tell by the look on Ship's face that he was.

"Your mama be moving like that?" he asked.

"Yep. Ain't that how it go? Ya mama is either a hoe or a fiend. What's yours?" I asked him.

"A fucking fiend." He shook his head.

"I'd rather mine be a fiend than a hoe," I remarked.

"You fucking bugging. That's easy to say when your mother ain't a fiend. Take it from a nigga that know. Your mother ain't hurting nobody by being a hoe."

"At least your mother has a reason. She's addicted. It's a

sickness. My mother just a horny ass bitch," I told him. "Ain't nothing stopping her from being better but her.

That was me and Ship's first real conversation. It was the first time I cooked for him. The first and second time we fucked. And the last time we would be apart until years later.

I treated my mother like the hoe she was until the day she died. Now that she'd been gone for years, I realize she was just as sick as Ship's mom. Heartbreak was a fucking disease. I knew firsthand.

Rhea not being Ship's daughter was heartbreaking for the three of us. He thought he was the only one going through it, but I was, too. My baby had the most perfect daddy. He was far from the perfect boyfriend, but he was a great father. Simply because he wanted to be. It got hard, but he never ran from the shit. He showed up for Rhea when he didn't have the energy to show up for himself.

I didn't know that Ship wasn't her father. I knew there was a possibility that he wasn't, but I moved on a hope and a prayer that we never had to find out. The day before I met Ship, Rhea's daddy shipped out for Missouri. We fucked all that morning and night. Then I met Ship, and we fucked all night. There was a fifty-fifty chance, but I wanted it to be Ship's. So, my scared ass tipped the imaginary scale to ninety percent in Ship's favor, regardless of the facts.

I let my anger get the best of me and blurted out that Ship wasn't Rhea's daddy, not knowing if it was true or not. In that moment, I wanted it to be true. Ship was controlling as fuck. He was so worried that Rhea had the hoe gene like me and my mother that he wouldn't let her do shit. I wanted to take my baby to the beach and put her in a pretty bikini. She didn't know shit about ass and titties; it was harmless.

That day was the bathing suit. But any other day of the week, it would be her hairstyles, her new earrings, a skirt she picked out of the store. It was always something. And it never failed; he always had to compare it to me being a hoe. I knew what I was, and I never denied it. But I was a damn good mother. My baby ain't want for shit. The both of us did for her. He always made it seem like he was the better parent.

We were on again, off again our entire relationship. When we were off, I did what the fuck I wanted, and so did he. But whenever he got mad, I was a hoe and Rhea would be one over his dead body. The shit was hurtful and constant as fuck. For him to keep repeating that shit at every disagreement told me that he didn't love me no more. He was with me because of Rhea. I just wanted him to leave me alone.

The second the shit left my lips, I knew it was the wrong thing to say. You couldn't take shit like that back. When Rhea came and told me about the game she played with daddy and her uncles, I knew it was a DNA test. He tried to say that he thought about it and didn't go through with it, but I wasn't stupid. I thought we could get through it but deep in my heart, I knew we never would.

Rhea's daddy, Fresh, didn't live in Baltimore anymore. His mother came to him randomly one day saying that they were moving to Missouri. Her goal was to get him out of the city. He was only here visiting because his mom's sister passed, and she didn't have a husband or a kid, so they were left to take care of her estate. They were packing up her house and putting it on the market.

He reached out with perfect timing, and we caught up. I hadn't even gotten the chance to tell him that Rhea was his daughter. He'd only laid eyes on her once, and that was only because he was leaving out just as my neighbor was coming home with our daughters from kindergarten. We had managed to fuck twice, but that was neither here nor there.

I went to meet Fresh outside when I heard him pulling up.

Rhea's nosey ass didn't miss a beat.

"Who he, ma?" Rhea moved her beaded lemonade braids from her face to peek at the door.

"DoorDash. I'll be right back," I told her.

Walking outside, I met Fresh at the trunk of my car. He noticed my expression and stopped in his tracks.

"Um," I bit my lip, sliding my hands into my back pockets. "Rhea is yours," I confessed.

His head whipped to my door. He moved closer, watching her through the screen.

"Mine?" he asked, glancing at me before focusing back on her.

"Yeah. She's yours. The day before you left for—"

"I remember," he said.

Fresh ran his hands down his face before walking over to me.

"Peaches, I'm engaged," he confessed. "I have my first kid on the way and—"

"That's funny because I just told you that Rhea is your daughter. So how can you have your first kid on the way?" I laughed in his face. "How are you in here fucking on me when you're engaged?" I asked him. "Where's your ring?"

"At the jeweler, getting refitted. I've gained a little happy weight," he said plainly like he didn't give a fuck about nothing I was saying.

"So, now what?" I asked, trying not to cry.

"You tell me. You're the one dropping this bomb on me." He threw his arms out.

"Yeah, like I've had anyway to contact you." I scrunched my

face up at him. "You left for Missouri and never looked back. Not so much as a phone call to say what's up," I reminded him.

"I heard about you fucking with somebody else not more than two days after I left. My first call home was to you and you ain't answer. I'm grateful that you didn't, though. I was a whole different nigga there. I ain't have to be no pants sagging, street hustling, wanna be gangsta. I'm Fresh because that's what my family calls me. Not because I'm somebody's fucking street thug. When I was Jace Anderson, you weren't that into me, remember?"

"That was what?" I tossed my arms up trying to calculate. "First grade, my nigga?"

"Yeah, and you ain't pay my ass no mind until I was in community college. Now you want me to what? Save you from this section eight apartment?" he asked. "I have a whole life in Missouri," he argued.

"So, what is this, some get back because back then I didn't want you?" I asked him for clarity.

"You not hearing me. It's not get back. I'm not hurt about it. I've done better for myself. My life is honestly fucking great. And while Rhea is a beautiful little girl, I can't just bring a child to my fiancée, who thinks we're both having our first fucking kid together." He put his hands to his head. "I'm sorry."

With that, he walked off. I stormed inside of my apartment, fighting the tears because I didn't what Rhea to see me crying.

"Mommy has to use the bathroom and then I'll be back to finish your hair," I told her.

When Fresh reached out, I thought it was a sign. Not that we could be together, but that he was here to take his rightful place as Rhea's father. It lined up perfectly with Ship and me going our separate ways and him telling me that he was going on a date and shit. The stars aligned too perfectly for this to be the result.

Fresh was an EKG technician making good ass money. He was just telling me that he purchased a house. He didn't mention the fiancée, who signed the deed with him. I don't know, I thought maybe Rhea and I would be moving to California. Shit didn't work out like that. And now Ship was heated with me for nothing. I had to fix shit with him. He was all my baby knew and apparently the only father she had.

Nevada

"You Nevada, right?" A stud girl asked me.

She had the attention of every nigga in here. It's not like we'd never seen one before. The girl was just pretty as fuck. Like, if she wasn't dressed like a nigga, had her hair styled like a nigga, we would've never known she was into girls. And she looked oddly familiar. I couldn't put my finger on it.

"Yeah, you tryna make an appointment?" I asked her, sipping the frozen lemonade that I got from Starbucks.

"Nah, I already made one."

"Oh, you're TJ?" I asked.

"Yeah." She nodded her head with a small laugh. "Expecting a man?" she asked.

"Well, yeah. You knew that though, right?" I called her out. "That's why you go by TJ."

"You right." She nodded her head with her hand to her chin. "Tell me something, Nevada. You like to get your pussy ate?" she asked.

The shop went silent.

"Check this." I moved her head to the side with the clippers close to her eyes. "I'm strictly dickly. You want to get a shape up, cool. But kill all that weird shit. I ain't with none of it, and neither is my nigga," I told her.

Ship ain't been my man officially but so what. It sounded

good as shit to say. That's when it hit me. She looked like a female version of my nigga. The more she talked, the more familiar her voice sounded. She was almost as smooth as him, too. Ship said he ain't have no family, though. It was just him. This bitch had to be his sister. She could go for his twin.

"Ard, ard." She put her arms up with a smile. "We good."

"That's what I thought."

It was back to business as usual. As the shop went back to their conversations, I got to know TJ better.

"You look mad familiar," I said to her. "You got a sister?"

"My grandma say I got a bunch of siblings scattered throughout this city and the next. I don't know none of them, though." she said.

"What ya mama and daddy got to say about that?" I pried.

"Don't know my mother. My father ain't told the truth since he was in the first grade. Some days he say yeah and some days, he tells me I'm the only thing he cares about, and other days, he's cursing me out because I can't give him some money or do something for him."

She was too forthcoming with information for me. I ain't really meet nobody in the city that just told all their shit like that. It was weird as fuck. But it was sounding like I was right. TJ was Ship's sister. What are the chances that I'd meet him only two seconds ago and make a connection to his sister? This shit was crazy.

"Check this shit. So last weekend, I told him I would work on his car and shit. For fucking free, mind you. This bitch brings the car to the shop with a flat tire. I'm thinking I'm just fixing his brakes. The nigga needed an oil change, his back tail light was out and some more shit. Motherfucker going to try and tell me that it wasn't like that when he dropped it off."

She even cursed like Ship. This had to be his sister.

"Have you ever tried looking for any of your siblings?" I asked TJ.

"Nah. I figure if they ever bothered to look, they'd find my grandma, if nothing else. But she ain't ever got no calls or nothing weird." TJ shrugged. "Plus, I'on know how they living. Motherfuckers might be living their best lives, and then my ass pop up to snatch it all away. Nah." She shook her head.

"Well, that could be true. What if they're living their worst life, though? They could be homeless. They might have mental health issues. They could even be living a good life and just be alone."

"Then I hope they find God like I did," she said.

"Not with the way you curse." I looked her up and down.

She laughed, getting out of the chair. "I just found him," she clarified. "And he knows my heart."

She had already paid on the website, but she tipped me twenty dollars anyhow.

"You got a business card?" I caught her at the door. "My car stay needing work, and you know how niggas do, trying to get over or get some pussy."

"Yeah." She nodded. "Follow me out to the car and I'll grab you one."

I hurried to grab my drink and rushed back outside. She was leaning in her car from the passenger seat. TJ and I said goodbye. It wouldn't be for long because I was taking Ship's ass to that shop for something. Reading her card, her real name was Tamiya Younger. If Ship just saw her, they'd both know that they were siblings. TJ said she just found God. He led her to me because he just led me to Ship. All I had to do was bring them together. The rest would happen naturally.

I went back into the store for my next client. Some nigga named Kong. Most of my customers were regulars. So, I always recognized a new name. He didn't use a last name, no real first name. The nigga ain't leave a real number. Nothing. But he paid, so whatever. He walked through the doors, amped up, dapping up half of the barbershop. They all addressed him as Kong.

He came straight to my chair and lifted his neck for me to snap the apron on. This nigga was rude as fuck. He ain't speak or nothing. He barely looked at me. Motherfucker just sat in my chair, holding conversations with half of the fucking barbershop. He needed the cut, though. Nigga looked like he'd been working in the fields all day. Not in a dirty way because he smelled good. Like Irish Spring soap. He had entirely too much energy for me. He was like an overactive toddler.

I did my best job, wanting to get him in and out of my chair. And I didn't want him complaining about shit either. Just as I was adding the finishing touches, Ship walked through the door with a plastic tray that I could only assume was for me. I cheesed immediately. And it disappeared just as quickly as Ship spoke to every nigga in the shop. He knew all these motherfuckers.

"What's up?" He walked over to me, grabbing me by my waist.

"You not funny," I whispered into his mouth, giving him a kiss.

"I brought you some lunch. Some of that good Jamaican shit." He placed the tray on the counter.

I opened it and took a bite.

"Ma'am, you not gonna finish my shit?" Kong looked back at me.

"My bad." I rolled my eyes when he wasn't looking.

I closed my tray and removed Kong's taper and the cape.

"Have a good day," I told him.

I turned back to taste my food, and Ship was already digging in my plate. I pouted and he fed me a piece of the oxtails and some rice.

"Hit my phone," Ship told me, kissing my lips.

"But I'm done with my customer," I whined. "I got like fifteen minutes."

"I gotta handle something with my brother."

Kong dapped Ship up when he was fully out of the chair. My mouth fell open. This motherfucker had too much shit with his ass. And damn, if I didn't love it. I guess that was his way of letting me, and these niggas in here, know he wasn't playing with my ass or theirs.

After fucking my food up, I had maybe five more heads before I was done for the day. I slid over to the school to pick Damari up, and we headed to McDonald's. It was never fast food when we went because Mari insisted on eating inside. I didn't mind it 'cause it allowed us to have dinner, lunch, and breakfast together like a family. It wouldn't be long before I was begging him to hang out with me. I appreciated these moments.

"Hello?" Mari answered his phone. "Hey, dad."

"Tell your father to call me tonight," I said. "I'm going to run to the bathroom and then we're going home," I told Mari as I ran off.

In the middle of me squatting over the public toilet, Siri started talking into my ear.

"Denver, red heart emoji is calling. Would you like me to answer it?"

"Yes, answer it," I responded.

"Answering now," Siri connected me to my sister.

"Hello?" I said into the phone as I flushed the toilet.

"Bitch, have some decorum. Don't answer the phone flushing the toilet," Denver said into the phone.

"Girl, this my shit. What the fuck you want?" I asked her. W

"You talked to Jemari, yet?" she asked, popping fucking gum in my ear.

"I just told Mari to tell him to call me tonight," I answered, drying my hands under the loud ass air dryer, knowing it would piss her off even more.

"Oh, damn." She sighed. "I was having a get together at my crib. I wanna meet Ship. But not if you ain't talked to Jemari because ain't nobody got time to make sure the two of you ain't in no pictures together," she said as I made it back to the table with Mari.

"I just told you that I'm talking to Jemari tonight. So, tell me the day and time and we in there," I told her.

"Bet. I just sent the invite."

"You could've said that shit over the phone." I glanced at the invitation. "And what the fuck is B.M.A.B?" I asked her.

"Bring me a bottle bitch. You know motherfuckers like to take their shit home. I'm done with those days. I'm paying for everything else. All motherfuckers got to do is show up, and they wanna be stingy with their bottles. Fuck that."

"Denver!" her raggedy ass boyfriend called her name.

I hung up on her before she could tell me she had to go. Denver always threw get togethers. I really hated her nigga, though. The only reason I still showed up to her shit was because I wanted to get a bird's eye view on what the fuck was really going on up in there. I sent Ship the invite.

Mari got out of his seat, sipping on his Hi-C, still talking to his dad. I took it that meant he was ready. We walked to the car, and I sped home. After a shower and a quick straightening up, Mari came into my bedroom.

"Dad said he's about to call you," Mari told me.

"Ok. Go on and get in the shower and put some pajamas on," I instructed.

"Ard." He rushed out of my room.

I had to catch him before he got caught up on that damn game. My mother suggested that I not allow him to get on the game on school nights. He never gave me trouble about getting up in the mornings, so I didn't see it as an issue. Adults had rules just to have them. Or, it was some shit their own parents did. I wasn't that parent. I was going to make sure the rules in my house fit my child.

For instance, the pantry was locked and stayed locked unless I unlocked it. If it wasn't, Mari's ass would eat all the damn snacks in one day. You ate what I made, or you ate a peanut butter and jelly. His room needed to be cleaned at all times. There was no Saturday morning cleanings because my shit was going to stay clean. He knew not to play with me about curfews, backtalking, or his chores. So regardless of what a motherfucker thought about my parenting, we had order around this motherfucker.

My phone rang, and my heart stopped.

Ship

I looked at the message Nevada just sent to me. It was an invitation to some game night shit. That wasn't my vibe, but I'd do that shit for her if she talked to her baby father like I asked her to. I had a lot of nerve because I hadn't said shit to Peaches yet. Ain't seen my baby in days. I talked to her on the phone, though.

Me, Kong, and Kiss were parked in front of Cambria's house. He was waiting on her and her friends to get to the house. One of them bitches was on the background of Cambria's live, talking about putting him on child support. He was tired of them bitches talking shit and tired of Cambria letting them.

We passed a blunt around the car for one of our confession sessions. It'd become a norm. The shit was kind of like therapy. Although we were all going to judge the fuck out of each other, we could be honest and get honest feedback in return.

"Ship, you talk to Peaches about Nevada yet?" Kiss asked from the passenger seat.

"Nah. I went to go talk to this bitch, and she had Rhea's daddy in there," I confessed. "Well, the nigga wasn't in there, in there, but he had her car and shit.

"It's her shit," Kiss stated the obvious.

"I don't give a fuck; he paid for it. She need to be respectful, the fuck?" Kong argued for me.

"What, she supposed to never move on? Only ride in the nigga car? He can't get in her shit, ever? What world do you niggas be living in? You can't give people shit and put limitations on what they do with it. You ain't wanna be with her, and she moved on. Tough shit, nigga," Kiss said.

"Yo, what the fuck is wrong with you?" I asked him.

The nigga was snappy in the house too. I know this Cambria shit wasn't getting under his skin that bad.

"Nothing," Kiss mumbled. "You niggas be mad about unrealistic shit. So what she had the nigga driving the car. You ain't making payments on that motherfucker. Shit be what it be, and y'all be wanting it to go your way. That ain't real life. You get what the fuck you get, and you play the damn hand," Kiss said, watching the parking lot.

"Nigga, shut the fuck up, 'cause we in the whip, waiting for Cambria to pull up with them dusty ass bitches she hang with," Kong spat.

"Because them bitches need to learn to mind their fucking business." Kiss spit out the window. "There they go," he said, waiting for them to park the car.

We all watched as Cambria's car turned off. One by one, Cambria and three of her friends piled out of her car. The three of us piled out right after them. Cambria noticed us, and they all ran towards the door like idiots. They made it inside, but they couldn't get the door shut. Kong pushed that motherfucker wide open.

"Which one of you bitches was on the internet talking about child support and shit?" Kiss asked as they all managed to find hiding spaces in the kitchen.

"It was fucking Zee." Brittany's big ass stood up from under the kitchen table.

"Bitch, why would you do that?" Zee snapped on Brittany.

"Because y'all always playing with this nigga gangsta. I

don't be involved in that shit, and I don't want the smoke behind it. I don't give a fuck." She sat at the dining room table.

"Kiss, we was just on there talking shit like we always do," Zee reasoned.

Kiss got right up in her face by the kitchen sink. He cut the water on and grabbed her by her head. "You bitches gon' stop speaking on me." He shoved her head under the sink like he was about to wash her hair.

"Kiss, let her the fuck go." Cambria tried to pull Kiss off of her, but it ain't work.

Kiss pushed Cambria and she flew to the floor.

"I don't know what that bitch done told y'all that got y'all thinking y'all can fucking play with me. But get that shit out y'all heads." Kiss looked at the other two while still wetting Zee's hair up. "I don't play with other nigga's bitches. You can call that nigga, your brother, your daddy. I don't got no picks. I'll beat the shit out of your grandmother if I feel like my life is on the line." Kiss shoved Zee's head away, and it hit the spout.

"You bitches and your fucking commentary on what the fuck Cambria should do when it come to me, be making me feel like my relationship with my kids is on the line. I'll murk all you bitches and won't think twice. I mean that shit," he warned them all. "And you," Kiss pointed in Cambria's face. "Stop fucking playing with me. I love the shit outta you, but I'll watch you breathe your last fucking breath behind my kids, bitch. They all I got!" Kiss barked in her face, making Cambria jump out of her fucking skin.

"And stop taking them to your fucking parents. They wanna see them, cool. But we don't need no fucking babysitters. Bring my kids to me, the fuck?" he said as he walked out of the kitchen. "Go get my babies, man, 'fore I pull up to ya mama house and pick them up myself," Kiss said, sitting down on the couch.

Nigga grabbed the remote, flicking the TV on.

"You in for the night?" Kong asked him.

"Yeah, I'll holla at you niggas," Kiss said, grabbing one of the couch pillows to lay his head against.

Kong and I walked to my whip.

"Something wrong with bro," Kong said.

"Hell yeah," I agreed as we pulled off.

You could feel the shit just being around him. He would've really killed all them bitches just now, including Cambria. I was trying to let the nigga talk when he was ready, but I was going to speak up before the nigga went out like Mont.

Peaches called me when I was around the corner from Kong's crib. I parked in front of his shit while we finished the blunt.

"You still not talking to that bitch?" Kong asked.

"Hell nah," I mumbled. "Fuck I'm supposed to say?" I shrugged.

"First, you tell that bitch that she gotta change Rhea's name," Kong said.

That shit had me dying laughing with his stupid ass. That was our shit, though. Tessa needed to change Raegan's name, too, shit.

"I don't even know what to tell you, nigga. You can't tell her ass about Nevada, though. And you definitely can't tell Nevada that you ain't said shit yet. You better lie to her ass and tell her that you talked to Peaches and shit is cool," Kong suggested.

"I ain't tryna go into this shit lying and all that."

"It's one lie, nigga. I lie to Schetta once a day. About dumb shit, too. It don't even matter." Kong shrugged. "She'll ask a nigga did he take the trash out. Like I know she see that shit sitting in there. So, I'll be like yeah. Then, when she catch me in the lie, I tell her I thought I did. Her ass think I'm retarded. My bad, mentally challenged. She don't like when I use that word." Kong shook his head. "This her big head ass right now. Watch this shit."

Kong put his Air Pods up and answered his phone on speaker.

"Hello?"

"Where you at?" Schetta asked.

"At my other baby muva house," he answered.

"Stop fucking playing with me. I see ya stupid ass outside with Ship," Schetta snapped.

"So why you asking me stupid shit? We kicking it. Give me a second," he told her.

"In a second, you gon' be on the couch. Bring ya ass in the house. Ask Ship if he wants a plate."

"Nah, I'm good, sis. Thank you, though." I called out.

"And you got me on fucking speaker?" Schetta was pissed. "So, I bet you be mad if I tell Ship how you be putting ya face—"

Kong hung up on her ass. "Let me get in this fucking house."

I laughed as we dapped up. Whatever Schetta was about to say scared his ass. That's why I wasn't excited about going to Nevada's for these toys and shit. I ain't know nothing 'bout no fucking toys. That shit was for bitches. Fuck around and let her ass try some shit, and she'd bring it up at the wrong damn time. And the wrong damn time was ever.

I headed to her crib anyway, still unsure if I was fitna lie or tell the truth about not talking to Peaches yet. If it came up, I was going with the first thing that came to my head. As I got out of the car, I texted Nevada that I was outside. I made my way up her building steps. The buzzer sounded, letting me know that she was letting me in.

I made my way to the third floor. The door of apartment C was cracked open, but I checked my texts again to make sure I had the right apartment. With confirmation that C belonged to Nevada, I took slow steps inside.

"Hey." Nevada smiled at me from the kitchen.

"What's up?" I asked, pulling my gun from my hip. "It smells good as shit in here," I told her.

"Thanks."

I started looking through the closet near the door. Next, I opened the half bathroom. That was clear. There was a shut door directly across from the kitchen on the same side of the door I walked through. I opened it and stepped in. It looked like it was for doing hair. I peeked into the closet, and there was a bunch of hair shit inside.

"Find anyone yet?" Nevada asked as I opened her pantry.

"Nope." I kissed her cheek, making my way through the rest of her apartment.

Niggas could never be too safe. My city was treacherous, and it ain't have no picks. You could be the man in the morning and be a dead man before lunch. Walking through her crib, I wondered how many niggas had done the same exact search in her shit. Bitch ain't even look up as I moved around her shit. It was clear that she was familiar with the procedure.

The last room I checked belonged to her son. The room was superhero'd out, from the ceiling fan, to the bedsheets, to the curtains. There was a single wall that looked like she'd paid someone to paint Superman there. The shit was about as tall as me.

"You son's room is dope as shit," I said, walking back into her kitchen.

On the outside of the kitchen were bar stools connected to the kitchen counter. I found myself a seat.

"Thanks. It was a waste of time because he's not into superheroes anymore. Everything is about sports. Thinking about basketballing it out, but I want to see how long he stays with it first."

"That's why you asked if I could hoop." I nodded my head.

"Yeah, I asked my son how he feels about me having a boyfriend." She glanced up at me, while she made my plate. "He's cool with it, but he made it clear that you not just gonna be in here fucking on his mama." We both laughed.

"He said that verbatim?"

I had to ask because my daughter ain't talk like that. And at seven, her son shouldn't be either. That was irresponsible as a parent. Nothing turned me off quicker than a mother who wasn't showing her kid the right shit. That's why I was always on Peaches's neck about the shit she was exposing our daughter to. She saw it as small shit, but kids picked shit up quick as a motherfucker. They wanted to make routines out of everything.

"No," Nevada snapped, offended. "He just asked if my boyfriend would take him fishing and take him to the court and shit." She shrugged. "You know, boy shit. I do shit with him, but he said it ain't the same." Nevada placed my plate down in front of me.

"If his daddy ain't got no issue, I don't." She took the fork she passed me.

"He doesn't," she said, standing at the counter, digging into the porkchops and onion gravy.

The mac and mashed potatoes were both homemade. She hadn't missed what I said about my favorite food. I ain't find no nigga or nigga shit in here. Her place was spotless. I could get comfortable over this motherfucker.

Nevada

"That means you talked to him about what we got going on," Ship said before stuffing some mac into his mouth.

"I did." I nodded my head. "I told him that I was seeing someone, and I was feeling the nigga. He asked if you had met our son yet. I told him no, but that it looked like things were going into that direction. We ended the conversation with him being cool with it," I said.

"That's it?" Ship asked with full on eye contact.

"Yeah, that's it. I told you me and my baby daddy ain't on that."

I knew Ship was looking for a lie, but that was the God's honest truth. The other shit Jemari said, Ship ain't need to know.

"What's up?" Jemari said when our call connected. "Mari said you wanted me to call you. So, I'm calling."

I could hear it all in his voice that he didn't want to talk to me. It was okay because I wished I didn't have to talk to his ass either. I would love to be petty and just pop out with Ship on social media like Jemari did me whenever he got new bitches. But I wanted to do everything with good intentions when it came to Ship and me. A part of that was the both of us respecting our child's other parent.

"I'm seeing someone and I'm really feeling him. I think this might be the real thing. It ain't feel right just popping out with a new nigga. Especially when you in that jail. Motherfuckers will tell you anything. I wanted you to hear the truth from me first. Not some shit

that was passed around twenty times before it made it to your ears," I said.

"He been around Mari yet?" Jemari asked.

"Nah. We not there yet. But I ain't gonna hold you. It looks like it's moving in that direction. I picked Mari's brain, and he cool with it. The nigga has a daughter, so he understands how that daddy shit works. He ain't tryna step on your toes."

"A nigga want you to be happy, Nevada. Even though I don't like your motherfucking ass ninety-nine percent of the time, a piece of me gon' always love you, even when I hate your ass. You tell that nigga who the fuck I am. Let him know that I don't play about you, and I will kill his ass behind my son. Long as that nigga respects that, we good," Jemari explained.

"Ard. Thanks for not going off. I ain't gon' hold you; I expected you to wild out a little." I laughed into the phone.

"I don't want your ass, girl," Jemari read my ass. "Aye, while you on here, my mama said—" he started, and I cut him off.

"Un-unh. I don't want to hear it. Whatever she wanted to say could have been said before I left her house. I'm good. Let's just gon' on and end this shit on a good note. I can already hear you fitna piss me off. Bye, Jemari." I hung up in his ear.

"Have you told your baby mother about me?" I asked, finishing up the last of my mac.

"Nah," he answered immediately. "I went to talk to her and some other shit popped up. I ain't speaking to her ass right now."

This should be red flag number two, but he told the truth. The nigga could have lied. But at the end of the day, he asked me to do something that he ain't done yet. It was half a flag.

"Can I ask what happened?" I pried.

"It ain't no shit I want to talk about right now. If I say that, then I got to get into other shit. And when that shit comes up, a nigga just wanna blow shit up," he explained.

I stared at him, wondering what the fuck he was referring to. He was probably one of those niggas who said he wasn't with his baby mother, but he still fucked on her whenever he wanted.

"Lemme guess. You doubled back and got her pregnant. Y'all not together, but she got a baby on the way somehow?" I rolled my eyes, clearing our plates from the counter.

"Fuck no! I don't touch that bitch. It ain't no me and her shit really. It's some me and my daughter shit. I ain't tryna get into it right now. But a nigga gon' let you know everything, just not tonight."

"Mmm," I moaned.

I pulled two glasses from my cabinet and the Disaronno from the freezer.

"Don't do that." Ship started pouring our drinks while I loaded the dishwasher. "A nigga tryna take his mind off that shit. It's all I think about. I just wanna have a night with my bitch."

I was trying to ignore the shit he was hiding, but it was hard. I felt like I was doing everything he asked. Both of my feet were in this. Ship only had one foot in. It was hard not to feel like I was getting played.

"How 'bout this?" He came up behind me at the counter. I grabbed my glass as he pressed his dick up against my ass.

"When's your sister's party?" he asked me.

"Exactly three weeks from today," I answered.

"By the time the party gets here, I'll talk to my baby mother, *and* I'll tell you why I'm not talking to her ass. If the shit ain't done, on my dick, you can cut a nigga off," he said.

"I'ma cut something off, ard," I mumbled.

"Damn." Ship took a step back from me. "You one of them?" he asked.

"I ain't the fucking two. Come on," I said, leading the way to my bedroom.

He didn't need any direction because the nigga had already scanned my entire apartment, closet to closet. That was advice I heard my mama give my stepbrother when he first started fucking. My stepdaddy preached condoms to him, and my mama warned him about triflin' women. Ship wasn't the first nigga to roam my shit like that, so I expected it. It came with the territory when you liked niggas with guns.

"I can smoke in here?" Ship asked as he came out of his shirt and jeans.

"Yeah." I climbed into the bed. "But I'd rather you get a pen for in the house." I pulled mine from my nightstand drawer.

"That's what I meant." He pulled one from his jeans pocket before getting on the bed.

We were laid up, watching a movie. The shit was good, and I wanted to see the end. But the weed and the drink, mixed with the energy coming from Ship's body had my pussy pulsating. I wanted that shit now. Pausing the TV, I got off the bed.

"You want a shot?" I asked, referring to his empty glass.

I'd just finished the last of my drink. A shot would put me where I wanted to be without making me feel like I needed to go to sleep.

"Of you," Ship answered.

"I be right back," my goofy ass giggled.

"Hurry up," he said.

And I did. I quickly took both glasses to the kitchen, poured myself a shot that I took standing right there, and stuffed the glasses into the dishwasher. I came out of my nighties in the kitchen and walked back into the room butt ass naked, tying my hair up into a ponytail.

"I'm ready for that dick," I told him.

"You ain't said shit."

Ship came out of his boxers. I hit the lights as he pulled his beater over his head. I flicked on my color changing light on his side of the bed. My room lit up in a royal purple. Ship could show me a good time. He knew how to flirt and get my pussy wet. The nigga didn't know shit about romance, though. I was going to have to teach him.

"Hey Siri, put on my Smoke with Me playlist on shuffle," I instructed her.

It was a playlist I started making after our first date. Every day since I added more songs. Some made me think about our future, others made me think about that dick. It was just our vibe. I ain't know if he listened to R&B or not, but he was going to learn to.

"Ok, now shuffling Smoke with Me from Apple Music," she responded.

Keyshia Cole's "Down and Dirty" came through the speaker in my light bulb. The lights began to flicker with the beat of the music.

"Damn."

I heard Ship mumble as I got on the bed and crawled my way to him. Like a lioness in the jungle, I eyed him until we were face-to-face. I put my lips to his mouth, and he leaned forward to kiss me. I slightly pulled away, making him bite his lips. His dick stood, poking me in my stomach. I built up the saliva in my mouth and let it drip onto his dick while staring into his eyes.

"Fuck," he mumbled, tossing his head back.

I circled my tongue around the tip of his dick. It started to flex in my hand. I inched him down my throat, coming up for air until I had all of him. Ship's body relaxed. He held the side of my face, moving his body up and down. I slurped the spit from his dick and let it drip again. His fist came down on the bed. He was restraining himself from busting in my mouth.

Ship sat up like something summoned him from a deep slumber. He could hear this pussy calling out to him. He lifted my face up. Gripping me by the throat, he pulled my face to his. Ship kissed the fuck out of me. He slapped my ass hard as fuck. A chunk of my ass cheek was in his hand. His finger played with the rim of my ass.

"Hold up," I told him.

I leaned over his leg and dug into my nightstand. That's where all my toys were. Whatever I was in the mood for was in that drawer. I pulled out a glow in the dark anal plug. I dipped it into my pussy as a lubricant. My juices glistened like diamonds as I passed it to him. He took it from my hands as I got in the sixty-nine position. Ship slid his body down so we were proportioned perfectly.

I bobbed my head up and down on his dick as he slid the plug into my ass gently. Immediately, the pleasure spread through my entire body. A bitch that didn't know this feeling was missing out.

Ship slurped my juices straight from my entrance before sucking on my clit like it was his favorite flavored Jolly Rancher. The more he sucked, the deeper I took him down my throat. My eyes were watering. My nose was running. His dick was marinating in my spit like a piece of meat. Bubbles began to form in various spots of his dick.

He nibbled on my clit, and that shit sent me over the edge. I humped his face until I was cumming in his mouth. Ship spread my cheeks, pulling me onto his tongue like he couldn't get enough. I sucked the tip of his dick as hard as he was sucking on my clit.

Ship

This was the first time that I had my tongue so far in a bitch pussy that I could feel her shit throbbing against my tongue. That plug turned her ass up a notch. Her being turned on was turning me on. That, mixed with the way Nevada sucked on my shit like she was trying to suck the motherfucker off, had me ready to buss.

"Chill, the fuck?" I smacked the shit out of her ass, gripping it like I could take some home with me.

Nevada laughed, rolling off of me.

"You not funny." I laughed with her.

I grabbed her by her ankle and dragged her down to me. She helped me lift her and sit her on my lap. My dick went right inside of her. It felt like I entered a fucking carwash for dicks or some shit. She flexed that water well against my dick as she moved her hips up and down. This bitch was nothing light. Tuning in to the music was helping to distract me from bussing. I was in a mental match with myself to not bust, stay up. A nigga was fighting that pussy. She was about to knock a nigga out.

I gripped her hips and controlled her motion, humping up into her, pulling her down firmly, quickly, slowly, then letting her do her thing for a few seconds. When a nigga was about to bust, I took control again.

"Ah, shit. Shit, shit, shit, don't stop. Right there," she moaned.

I gripped her by her neck, continuing to hump into her the way she wanted. As she came, her eyes opened. The shit looked like something out of a fucking scary movie. I was about to die in this room, because I couldn't pull out of her ass.

Nevada stared into my eyes, a tear dropped, and it was over.

"Oh, shit," I moaned.

One hand on her throat and the other on her hip, I bust all in that pussy. That motherfucker was mine, whether she wanted it to be or not.

"Fuck!" I let her out of my grip.

"Whew, shit." Nevada said, falling flat onto my chest.

I kissed her forehead twice while she gripped me at my side.

"I don't fight bitches over dick. Never did. But a bitch will have to put me in a grave for me to come up off that motherfucker," Nevada said.

"Same," I told her.

We both bust out laughing. I pulled her hair from her ponytail, playing in its length. She traced my tattoos with her fingers.

"You on birth control?" I asked her.

"Yea. I don't think that's enough for the nut you just bust inside of me, though. I'm going to get a Plan B in the morning," she said.

"It wouldn't be the end of the world if you didn't," I told her.

"Huh?" She lifted her head up fast as fuck.

"I don't know." I ran my hands down my face. "A nigga might be pussy whipped. Saying anything," I looked at her.

That post-nut clarity had me ready to walk down the aisle

with her ass. I wanted everything she had to offer, including that womb that could house a kid with my blood. If what she said about her baby father being cool with shit was true, then she was one of them cool ass baby mamas. If shit didn't work out with us, it wouldn't be no crazy ass toxic shit. We could co-parent and still be cool.

That nut showed me a whole bunch of shit. And I ain't see us being apart after tonight. I just wanted to be up under her ass.

"We don't even know each other like that," she answered.

"So what?" I shrugged.

I grabbed my phone from the nightstand. The urge came over me to call Peaches and tell her about Nevada. I didn't give a fuck if Nevada did go back to her baby father. We were just going to have to share her ass. Fuck that.

"Who are you calling?" Nevada asked, sitting up.

"Hello?" Peaches answered the phone.

"Aye, look," I started. "I'm seeing somebody. I fuck with her. I'm still going to do everything for Rhea that I do now. This don't change that. But a nigga got a bitch now," I said, ending the call with Peaches.

"Why would you do that like that?" Nevada snapped, getting off of the bed.

"Why it matter how I did it? I did the shit." I shrugged.

"And you think that makes it easy for me to occupy a space in your life, for real?" Nevada cut the music off and flipped the lights on. "Like I want to meet your daughter. If we doing this relationship shit, for real, I want our kids to be close, like siblings. Dropping a bomb on your baby mother like that ain't making our shit easy. It's complicating it more," she argued.

I watched Nevada gathering things for a shower. She was

fitna go wash my nut outta her. I wasn't joking 'bout shit. A nigga wanted another kid. And I wanted Nevada to be the mother. I wanted to see her ass every day and every night for the rest of my fucking life.

"She ain't my baby mother," I confessed.

"What?" Nevada scrunched her face up.

"A little over a year ago, me and the bros did one of those at home DNA test joints," I started. "The shit came back that Rhea isn't mine."

A nigga's eyes started to water. If I thought about the shit, I couldn't keep my composure. Every time I had to say the shit out loud, I lost control. That shit hurt so fucking bad, still.

"She still my baby. But every time I look at her, I'm reminded of that damn test. When I went to talk to Peaches the other night, some nigga was out with her car. The car I bought. A nigga may have been tripping off that. Like, it's her car now, fuck it. But when she told me it was Rhea's real dad, I lost it. I am her real father. Rhea don't know that nigga. And I don't know shit else. She the only blood thing I got on this earth."

Nevada came and laid in my arms. I don't know if she was deciding that she was going to let that nut travel to her cervix or if she just forgot because she felt bad for a nigga. Either way, she was laid up under me, right where I wanted her. The shit sounded crazy as fuck, but for me, it felt right. I wanted a kid.

"You think you can go to the car shop with me tomorrow?" Nevada asked. "You know how they be trying bullshit when women go by themselves."

"I'm all yours," I mumbled, ready to knock out.

∞∞∞

At the car shop the next morning, I stood behind Nevada as she talked to the nigga behind the desk.

"Hi, is TJ here?" she asked.

"Nah, she don't work weekends. What you need?" dude asked.

"Thanks," Nevada said, leading the way outside.

I followed her back to her car, wondering what the fuck was going on. If she knew somebody who worked here, why the fuck she need me to come with her? I thought I was coming so these niggas ain't try to overcharge her for some shit she didn't need. If she wanted to be a passenger princess, she could've just said that.

Watching her juicy ass thigh slip into the passenger seat, my mind hadn't changed at all. I hoped one of my swimmers was already attaching itself in that motherfucker. On the way here, I waited to hear her ass ask me to take her to a CVS or some shit, but she hadn't. So, we were both on the same page.

"If you just wanted a nigga along for company, you could've just said that." I started the car up.

It was nearing summer and showing in the weather. It was too hot to be chilling in the car with no A/C bumping.

"Ard, so, I really wanted to stay out of it and let y'all come to y'all own conclusion, but the TJ I asked about?" I nodded my head that I was following her. "That's your sister."

"The fuck is you on? A nigga ain't got no sisters. No daddy, no mama, just brothers that ain't no kin to me on paper."

That was one of the first fucking things I told her ass. I know I said the shit to her at least twice. Bitches ain't listen for shit.

"I know what you said, but I know what the fuck I know.

This girl is your fucking sister. She looks like your twin, and she has the same last name," Nevada argued.

"You know how many Youngers there are in Baltimore?" I asked her with my face scrunched up.

"But she told me a little bit of her story. She was raised by her grandmother. Your father's mother."

"I don't got no fucking father, Nevada. You fitna piss me the fuck off, for real."

"Well, ya sperm donor's mama." Nevada sucked her teeth. "And she knows she has siblings but ain't met none of them. You are one of them. I can call her right now so you can see for yourself. You done told me over and over that you ain't got no blood. You do. Everybody got blood. And you could meet them if you trust what I'm saying," she pleaded. "This girl is your sister."

I considered what she was saying. A nigga could have legit family out this motherfucker. I might've fucked on my cousin and ain't know it or some shit. It was never on my mind to look for my father or his peoples. Any nigga bussing in my fiend out ass mother wasn't worth shit. I never cared to meet his ass. Having siblings never crossed my mind. It'd always been just me and my brothers.

Nevada hadn't brought me a bag thing yet. I genuinely felt like she was bringing me all the good shit in the world. But this wasn't about trusting her and her intentions. This was about the chances that this TJ bitch was really my sister. I ain't want to open no more doors that were going to be shut in my face later. I had my brothers. I had Rhea. And now I had Nevada and hopefully another baby. I hadn't met her son yet to say I had him, but once I met the little nigga, I'd have him, too. A nigga was good with that.

"Nah, I'm not interested," I told Nevada as she typed quickly on her phone.

Nevada looked at me and bit her lip. "I already told her to meet me here. She's on the way."

I twisted my lips up at her, shaking my head. "Let me find out you one of those *Moesha* ass bitches, always in somebody fucking business, thinking you helping and really fucking shit up."

"I don't fuck shit up. I fix. If this ain't your sister, on my mama, I will suck your dick every day for the rest of our lives." Nevada leaned over, kissing me.

"You was going to do that anyway," I told her.

We fell into laughter, but a nigga was nervous as shit. I didn't know if I was more worried that TJ was really my sister or that she wasn't. I didn't want to get my hopes up. But a nigga couldn't convince his body or brain to play this off as some light shit. I might have a fucking sister, bruh. What the fuck?

TJ

"Now where you taking me, girl? You said we was going to Golden Corrals. I don't know what Golden Corrals you going to," my grandmother talked her shit.

"It ain't no *S* on the end of it," I told her. "I gotta make a stop at the shop real quick. We still going out to eat. Relax, big back," I joked with her.

"You know who got a big back? Your motherfucking mama. I thought ya daddy was bringing a fucking elephant through my door when I met her. That ugly ass bitch could've stuffed a roast in between her rolls," Grandma shot back at me.

I died laughing while she was still mean mugging like I did something to her. She'd talk shit about my mother all the time. All I knew about my mother is she was ugly, fat, and stupid. And I learned all that from the shit my grandmother talked about her.

Grandma said she knew I was one of them because of my fingers. Apparently, we had moles on our wedding fingers. A long line of women who'd never been married. She said we were destined to be baby mothers, mistresses, and long-term girlfriends. I was going to prove her wrong with that one. A good woman would find me and when she did, I was going to marry her. I hoped it was my current girl, but it was feeling it wasn't. I told Grandma that too, and she said it didn't count 'cause girls can't marry girls.

She accepted that I was a lesbian. In fact, she's the one

who told me I was when I was coming out to tell her. She said, "If you'd stopped acting like you liked dick, you'd be a whole lot happier." And my sexuality was never a conversation again. She still gave her unsolicited advice when I ran into relationship hiccups. I took her words with a grain of salt because she never had nothing nice to say about a woman.

"And you better make this shit quick," Grandma said, as I pulled into the parking lot.

I would've preferred to come alone. Grandma was already in my car when Nevada hit my phone. I was tryna holla at her fine ass. She could talk all that shit about not being into girls, but two of the women I loved had said the same exact thing. It was nothing to turn a woman out. They never knew what they wanted until it was staring them in their face.

"It'll only take a second," I told her as I got out of the car.

I didn't have to look around for Nevada because she hopped out of a car when she spotted me. But she got out of the passenger seat. I glanced at her driver's seat, and it was some yellow nigga sitting there, eyeing me.

"Hey, so, I didn't call about my car," Nevada started.

I looked her up and down. The way this woman made a pair of Dunks look like high fashion was insane. It didn't matter who she came with. I knew I could sway her to come to the slippery side. That yellow nigga got out of the car and made his way over to where me and Nevada stood.

"I'm not understanding," I said, confused.

It was feeling like a setup. I knew better than that. I'd found God with a clear conscience. All my debts were paid in full. All my beefs in the streets were settled. I didn't have to look over my shoulder anymore. None of that had turned my street sense off, though. This wasn't violence. But it wasn't peace either. Something weird was going on.

The sound of a car door slamming made me look behind me. Grandma was getting out of the car, walking towards us. She acted like she'd been waiting on me for hours.

"Who ya mama, boy?" she said, looking at the yellow boy who slid out of the driver's seat.

"Nadine," he answered.

"Brown skin, skinny thing. Got more mouth that a fucking chihuahua?" Grandma asked.

"Yes ma'am," the dude answered with half a smile. His eyes watered as he nodded his head. Nevada started smiling hard as shit.

"I'm ya grandmother, nigga. Welcome home." She reached her arms out to him.

Damn. This yellow nigga was my brother. Younger brother it looked like. I guess that was it for my plans to snatch Nevada from her man. Grandma was whispering something into the yellow nigga's ear. He was crying uncontrollably as she rubbed his head and rocked him back and forth like a baby. I knew what he was feeling, wrapped up in her arms because Grandma had done me the same way the first time I met her.

I remember her every word verbatim. *"You home now. Home is wherever Grandma is. I loved you before I knew you because I knew you were out there. You don't worry about who didn't love you. Fuck who didn't want you. Grandma love you. Grandma want you. You ain't ever got to worry about another motherfucker again, you hear me?"* I never forgot that. And whenever I find myself in something, I let her words play.

"Hey, sorry I kind of ambushed you." Nevada walked over to me with an innocent smile.

"You saying sorry and I'm saying thank you," I told her.

"You're welcome." Nevada smiled at me, staring at her

man.

Ship was sobbing into Grandma's arms. I walked over to join them.

"What's up, man. TJ." I held my hand out to him, introducing myself.

"Ship." He wiped his eyes before dapping me up.

"Welcome home," I told him.

"Thank you." He nodded his head.

Nevada walked over and Ship wrapped his arm around her neck, placing several kisses on her forehead.

"And who is this heffa?" Grandma asked.

"Please, don't take no offense. She just say whatever comes to mind. She don't mean no harm, I swear," I warned them about Grandma.

"Don't be apologizing for me. I asked who the girl was, shit."

"Her name is Nevada. This my girl. She set all this up," Ship said.

Grandma looked at her for a little while. Nevada and Ship stood around awkwardly, waiting for something.

"Well, ard." She nodded her head. "We was on our way to the buffet." Grandma always pronounced the *T*. Y'all follow us down there. Come on," she said, walking off to the car without waiting on an answer from either of them. "Taniya, bring ya ass," she called out to me.

"I guess we'll see y'all there?" I asked, walking backwards to my car.

"Right behind you," Ship said as he and Nevada got in the car.

It wasn't a secret I had siblings out there. For some reason, I thought I'd go through life never meeting them. Baltimore was big, but it was small as fuck. Everybody knew somebody who knew somebody who knew somebody. People were too consumed in themselves to be worried about who the next person knew. Nevada must've really loved my brother. She was paying attention to him. If I couldn't have her, at least my brother could.

It didn't feel weird saying "my brother" because he was. The same way my grandma loved me before she met me. I loved all my brothers and sisters. It didn't matter if I didn't know them. One day I would—even if it wasn't until we made it to heaven.

Grandma didn't say much on the ride. She was on her phone, playing solitaire.

"Grandma?"

"Not right now, Taniya. Hush, girl," she said.

I only wanted to ask her if she was going to tell Ship about Pat, and if she was going to ask Pat about Ship. He came around here and there, but Grandma refused to talk to him. Like ever. He couldn't even get a "hello" from her. But she never turned him away. She didn't encourage him to stay either. I spoke to him because he was still my father. He wasn't the one I wanted, but Pat was the only one I had.

When we pulled up to the buffet, Nevada and Ship got out of the car. He walked over to her side of the car. They were hugged up, kissing, when Grandma interrupted them.

"You got kids?" she asked Nevada as we all walked through the front door.

"Just one," Nevada answered.

"You gonna have another one if you don't let the boy

breathe for a second," Grandma said as I led the way inside.

I think she had it wrong this time. It was Ship who was all over Nevada. I couldn't blame him. I wouldn't go at her outta respect for him, but I was human at the end of the day, and I liked women. I was going to look.

"And you," she said to Ship. "What ya mama name you? I'm not calling you no gahdamn Ship. Even Ships have names."

"Patrick," she answered.

"Ya mama's a stupid bitch. You know that?" Grandma said, frankly. "Gonna name you after a nigga that ain't give a fuck about her and even less about you," she said as I pulled her chair out. "What you doing?" she asked me.

"Pulling your chair out, like I always do." I scrunched my face up at her.

"You's a girl, Taniya. Your brother got it from here," she told me.

I laughed, putting my hands up in the air and finding a seat. It wasn't like it was some shit I wanted to do anyway. I did it out of respect for her being my grandma. Ship could have that responsibility. I agreed with Grandma. Pulling out chairs was for gentlemen. I was a woman.

Ship pulled her chair out and found a seat. The waitress came over and took our drink orders.

"Now, you come with me so we can get our plates," she said to Nevada. "Let these two go up together so they can get to know each other," Grandma said, getting up from the table.

We all complied like she was a Sergeant, and we were the soldiers.

"Grandma talks a lot of stuff, but she's harmless," I told Ship as we grabbed plates.

"She reminds me of my homeboy's grandmother. I'm used to it. Missed it for real."

"Well, she never turns it off. Some days, I don't be in the mood, and she don't care nothing about that. I try not to let it make me mad. If I don't know nothing else about her, she going to be consistent. She doesn't change."

"I'm not a fan of change," Ship said. "Is it more of us?" he asked.

"Yeah, but I don't know how many. I never met any of them. Just you," I told him.

"You always lived with her?" Ship asked me.

"Nah," I responded. "That's a long and ugly story. We should link after this. Tell all of our long and ugly stories. It's been just me and Grandma since I was eighteen. So, I'm feeling good about having a brother," I told him.

"I ain't got a blood nothing. So, I'm just happy to find out it's not just me," he said.

We walked around the buffet, stacking our plates like there wouldn't be seconds. When we made it back to the table, Grandma started talking.

"The whole car ride, I was in my head, trying to remember what I could about ya mama," Grandma said. "It's up to you if you want to hear it or not," she offered.

That was one thing about Grandma. She always gave you an option. I couldn't remember a time where she forced me to learn some shit about either of my parents. If I asked, she'd tell me. But she never just tossed no shit out there at me.

Nevada

On the ride home, I was so pissed with Ship. When his grandmother asked him if he wanted to know about his mom when she was pregnant, his ass said no. Like, what the fuck was that? Why wouldn't he want to know more about his mother? Then, she asked if he wanted to know about his father. He told her that she and TJ were enough. He didn't want to talk about nobody who wasn't there.

We hardly talked in the car. I don't think he could tell that I was mad at him. So, that had me thinking that he was mad at me. When we pulled up at my house, Ship wasn't walking up the steps with me.

"I be back, ard?" he said to me.

"Like right back or next week?"

I didn't like that he was playing word games. Niggas always found a way around some shit. I wanted clear and concise language so there was no confusion. He wouldn't be able to hit me with bullshit later.

"I wanna see my daughter. I be back after that," he said, grabbing my hand and pulling me back down the steps.

"Ok." I nodded, and he gave me a kiss.

I couldn't be mad at that. When I was going through something, the only thing I wanted was my son. I thought it was honorable that Ship still wanted to be in Rhea's life after finding out he wasn't her dad. If I was being honest, I didn't think it was realistic. Not if he wanted us to be together like he said.

There wasn't much I knew about his and Peaches relationship. I knew her name, his daughter's name, and those were facts. The information I gathered is that Peaches still wanted to be with Ship. And if I knew nothing else about a woman, she was going to use Rhea to make Ship jump. I couldn't understand why he thought he had the upper hand. At the end of the day, Rhea wasn't his.

I wasn't sure what I was thinking skipping over a Plan B. I didn't know this nigga enough to be fucking him raw to begin with. Honestly, I wanted another kid. Ship wanted to take care of a kid that wasn't even his because he loved her that much. Our kid would be his. That had to guarantee that he would be around, even if shit fell flat with us.

I didn't want to sit in the house. I would end up waiting around on Ship, clutching my phone in my hand. It wasn't out the norm to pop up on my sister. I called Mari on the way over, just to hear his voice. He stayed with my parents every other weekend at the request of my stepdad. My parents helped with my stepbrother's daughter while he was overseas, and his wife was pregnant again. My mom was done with raising kids, but my stepdad argued that it wasn't fair to get one grandkid and not the other. So, every other weekend, I was kid free.

"Mari, I'm going to pick you up in the morning. Go have fun with your cousin. I love you," I told him as I pulled into the Walgreens parking lot.

"I love you, too, ma."

I hung up and ran into the store. There was still time for me to take a Plan B. I rushed around the store like Ship would catch me in there. Checking out, I stuffed it into my purse and headed to my car. I didn't just want one more kid. I wanted five in total. Demari, Rhea, whatever Ship put in me last night if it stuck, and that meant he would owe me two more. Because three baby daddies wasn't an option and neither was Jemari. Ship and I were going to talk tonight when he got back from seeing Rhea.

I pulled up in front of my sister's. From the car, I could hear Denver yelling. I ran up the stairs like Sha'Carri Richardson. Banging on her door, I screamed her name.

"Denver!" I started knocking on windows.

Her dusty ass boyfriend snatched the door open. I looked him and down before moving past him.

"You can speak or get the fuck out," Vince barked on me.

"Nigga, please," I said, running up the steps to find my sister.

It was a townhouse that my daddy got her, and Vince's bitch ass wasn't even supposed to be staying there. He had me fucked up and so did Denver.

"I know this nigga not living here," I said, as I stepped into her bedroom.

"He here every day, might as well be," she mumbled, cleaning up the mess in her room.

There were clothes flung all over the place, cups knocked over, a tequila bottle dripping onto the floor. The TV was broken, and there was a hole in the wall right above her bed.

"Daddy gon' go the fuck off when he see how fucked up this place is." I looked around at the mess.

"Daddy ain't going to find out because you ain't going to say shit," Denver snapped.

"Bitch, what the fuck do y'all got going on in here?" I asked her.

My sister could handle herself. I was the one who came and got her when bitches tried to jump me. You couldn't say shit to me without me going to get my big sister. But Nae dying really changed her. This bum ass nigga Vince really changed her.

"Regular shit. He don't be knowing who the fuck he talking to," she said.

"I know because I came in this bitch and he gon' tell me to speak or get the fuck out," I told her.

"What?" She scrunched her face up and ran down the steps.

I was right behind her. They already had too much going on. Under normal circumstances, we'd beat his ass together. But this shit was different. I didn't need proof to know Denver would stay with his ass anyway.

She moved around the first floor, looking for Vince, but he wasn't here. Denver looked out the window for his car. "Oh my God." She ran over to the door. "I'm so sorry, Nevi," she said with her hands over her mouth.

I ran to the door to see my entire front windshield was shattered.

"Sorry?" I asked her. "Bitch, look at my fucking window!" I yelled at her, running down her front steps to my car.

She was on my heels, calling Vince over and over again. The fuck was that going to do but get his bitch ass killed? My first mind said to call my daddy. Either one of them. That would only have me and my sister going at it. Vince wasn't trying to do shit but isolate her from me. I was her only confidant. He wanted me away from her.

I reached out to insurance to file a claim. They told me that the earliest someone could come and fix the window was three days from now. I was so pissed. I took every expensive item out of my car and put them in plastic bags that Denver had gotten out of her house.

"You sure you don't want me to just run you home?"

Denver asked.

"No."

I was too pissed off to give her anything but yes or no answers. Everything else I ignored. If she wanted to be with this stupid nigga, cool. But when her bullshit started to spill into my life, that was a fucking problem.

"Well, at least come in the house and wait for Ship," she suggested.

"No."

I didn't want to be in her shit. I didn't want to be around her. She could take her goofy ass in the house and wait for that nigga to come home. Denver needed to get the fuck away from me.

"I know you ain't trippin' on me 'cause of some shit another nigga did," Denver said, punching her fist in her hands.

"Go the fuck 'head, bruh," was the only warning I was giving her.

I heard Ship's car before I saw it. He had the most perfect timing. Somebody was going to have to pull me off Denver's ass if she didn't take her ass in the house.

"I'm not going nowhere. You not fitna put that shit on me. First off, you popped up at my shit unannounced like you always do. Secondly, you walked into *his* shit and didn't speak."

Ship double parked. I beelined straight to his car. I could feel Denver on my heels.

"Back the fuck up," I said, swinging the car door open to put my things inside.

"Woah," I heard Ship say before getting out of the car.

"And what the fuck you think you 'bout to do?" Denver

asked him. "You can stay ya ass over there. I'm talking to my sister," she told him.

"Hold the fuck up." I slammed his door shut, making my way to Denver. "Don't talk to my nigga like that. He's making sure I'm good."

"That's what I'm trying to do, but you being all weird like I'm the one that bust your fucking windshield."

"Your nigga did!" I yelled in her face.

"Get the fuck out of my face, Nevada," Denver warned me.

"Or what, bitch?" I moved closer.

Ship scooped me up in his arms and put me in the passenger side of the car. He shut the door, and I rolled my window down.

"When that nigga start beating your fucking ass, don't call me, bitch!" I yelled out of the window.

Ship sped down the block and turned.

"What the fuck y'all got going on?" he asked.

"Do you want a baby, for real?" I asked, snapping on him.

"How the fuck I get in this? Cut that attitude shit the fuck out. I came and rescued you. Why you giving me all that static?" Ship talked with his hand on his chest, glancing back and forth between me and the road.

"Rescued? I could've called a Lyft," I told him, grabbing my purse from between my feet.

"But you didn't. You called me. You wanted me. And I came straight to you, no stops. So, chill."

I pulled the Plan B from the plastic bag and started ripping the box open.

"I want five kids. I have one. You have one. That's two. I

want three more. If you ain't tryna give me three more, we can dead this shit right here," I told him with the pill in my hand.

This wasn't how I planned to have this conversation. But I didn't plan to be pissed off when I saw him. So, it was what it was.

"Take that shit, and it'll be a waste of your time 'cause I'm nutting in you tonight." He shrugged.

"So, five kids?" I asked, surprised that he agreed.

"Five kids," he told me at the red light.

He rolled the window down and I tossed the pill out.

"You hungry?" he asked.

"For dick."

I leaned over, undoing his jeans. I pulled his dick from his boxers and sucked him like he would fill me up.

Ship

A nigga can't say he ain't got no blood no more. I got a whole sister. Well, a half-sister, but that shit didn't matter. I already loved her on the strength.

Soon as Grandma asked who my mama was, I knew I was hers. She told me that, too. That initial hug had a nigga choked up but when she started talking in my ear, she took me under.

"Grandma got you now, baby. I might curse you out, I might beat you across your head, but Grandma here for as long as God allow me to be. You ain't got to worry about nobody that didn't want you. Fuck who didn't love you. I love you and everything that come with you. You hear me?"

I couldn't even say "yes ma'am" because I couldn't catch my breath. My chest was tight. My stomach was full of...I don't even know what to call it. I guess happiness. A nigga felt lighter. Like the pain I'd been carrying around had been lifted a little.

I was going to see my grandma tonight, and I had a dinner with Nevada's peoples. It was different to have so much going on, but I liked it. All family shit, too. I couldn't wait for the holidays and all the ripping and running I would have to do. It was wild how life could really change overnight.

Me and the bros were on break at work. Kiss wasn't saying much, still. Nigga was deep in his head about something. Kong was getting as impatient as I was about it.

"If you fitna go out like Mont, just say that shit, nigga. So, we can get prepared," Kong spat.

"Shut the fuck up, bitch. A nigga got shit going on. Shit I ain't tryna talk about. I'll never go out like that nigga. I got kids, bitch," Kiss argued.

"That's what you trippin' on?" I asked Kiss. "Mont?"

"Nah, I'm over that shit. Well, I ain't over it, but what a nigga supposed to do?" Kiss shrugged. "The shit with Tessa fucked up but again, what a nigga supposed to do? I got shit going on that I don't want to talk about, but a nigga ain't fitna crash out," Kiss assured us.

"Well, ard, then." Kong said, crunching on a piece of chicken. "I think Schetta drinking again," Kong admitted.

"Boy, that girl ain't touched no damn bottle," Kiss snapped on him.

"Then she pregnant." Kong shrugged. "Her sneaky ass is up to something. Keep disappearing with her aunts and shit. Kong wiped his mouth with a napkin. They doing all this fucking hanging out. I'ma catch her little ass. She gon' be looking like a deer in headlights." Kong tossed his leftovers in the trash.

"Nigga, that girl ain't doing shit," I told him.

Schetta worshipped the ground that Kong walked on. The nigga could breathe just a little too hard, and she'd be asking if she needed to make him a doctor's appointment. I didn't see her hiding a pregnancy. Her happy ass would be telling the world by now. That shit was either in his head or it was something else.

"Y'all tryna hit the casino tonight?" Kong asked as we walked outside for break.

"Nah, I'm going to see my grandma," I told him.

"Look at this nigga," Kong said to Kiss. "Boy happy as shit he got a grandma." He laughed.

"Nigga got a Kool-Aid smile like a dog at a dog park," Kiss

added.

"Fuck y'all niggas." I laughed them off. "I'ma bring y'all to meet her soon. I don't mind sharing her with y'all," I told them as I dipped off to my department.

Unlike Kong and Kiss, I worked in the packing department. A nigga stood in the same spot all day, packing or bagging out orders. Back at my workstation, I set my phone on the shelf and FaceTime Nevada.

"Hey, babe. You better not be calling to cancel dinner with my parents." She gave me the side eye.

"Nah, man. Why you keep thinking a nigga is ducking and dodging ya family? I'm not scared of them people, girl. I was calling to get the time again."

"It's at eight, Ship. How many times do I have to tell you that?" she snapped on me.

"Aye, cut that attitude shit. I'm just tryna make sure I got the shit right, so I can be there for you. Why you trippin' on a nigga for?" I asked her as I packed a blender into the shipping box.

"My bad." She bit her lip. "I'm just a little nervous. I ain't brought a nigga around them since my baby daddy. It's stressing me out."

"And you stressing me out. It ain't that serious. We gon' do this little dinner shit with ya peoples, and then I'ma take you home and fuck the shit out of you."

"Ard." Nevada pouted. "Lemme take care of this client, and I'll call you later," she told me.

I ended the call, feeling seen by enough of them niggas. It wasn't that I didn't trust Nevada. I didn't trust them niggas in that damn barbershop. I ain't want her working in there but wasn't shit I could do. Nevada said that was how she made her money and unless I wanted her taking house calls, this was what she had to do.

After work, I was in and out of the shower. I jumped in the car and headed to Grandma's house.

When I was younger, I used to fantasize about someone coming to fucking save me from my mother. I'd be in a store, minding my business and a stranger would walk up to me, asking me if I was my daddy's son. It would turn out to be an aunt or an uncle. They'd take me home, and family would be lined up to meet me. The vision never changed.

Eventually, I convinced myself that no one was coming to save me from her. I was going to have to do that shit myself. I'd put on the bummiest shit I owned, trying to get a motherfucker to care enough. It took no time because Kiss's mom and Kong's mom got me right.

When Kiss's parents took him school shopping, they took me, too. His mama and Kong's mama made sure I ate every day. Most of all, they made sure I didn't end up in the system—even if it meant they had to come clean my mama house because she had a DFS visit coming.

I had a lot of people who stepped up for me. They'd be my family forever, blood or not. But a nigga would be lying if I said that was enough. It's nothing like knowing where you came from. Project baby or not, that two parent household showed on Kiss. He was damn near the only nigga in the projects with both parents, and they weren't no triflin' motherfuckers. Even when they put him out, they still looked after him.

I always wanted that. Not in a jealous way because Kong and Kiss shared everything they loved with me, except their bitches. But all I ever had was them. I would love them niggas and their families forever. I just wanted my own family, too.

I rushed up the front steps and knocked on the door. I was

anxious to get inside. I knew there wouldn't be a shit load of family waiting for me on the other side of the door. They told me at the dinner that it was just the two of them. Little did they know, that was more than I ever thought I would have.

"What's up?" TJ dapped me up as I walked through the door.

I might as well have walked into a museum. That's what it felt like. It wasn't huge with large ceilings. No paintings by famous artists. But this was my first time in my grandmama house. Her couch, her carpet, her everything. It felt like I was in the home of a dead celebrity. I didn't want to touch anything. I was scared it would break. Or somehow, my fingerprints would damage it. Reality was this would not be my last time here. But I wanted to take it all in. This was a piece of Grandma's personality. A part of her I hadn't gotten to know yet.

"You good? Want some water or something?" TJ asked me.

"Nah, why you say that?"

"You look like you just seen a ghost." TJ laughed.

"Something like it. I'm good, though," I told her.

"You want a tour?"

"Hell yeah." I followed her lead up the steps.

"Ard, so this is grandma and her parents. These are her siblings, but they are all gone now." TJ pointed to pictures on the wall as we went further up the steps. "This was Grandma's trick."

"Huh?"

"Grandaddy. I never met him. But she said he wouldn't marry her. He bought her everything she wanted. So, he was her trick." TJ shrugged. "I couldn't even argue with her."

Me and TJ hollered. She walked me through the rest of the upstairs before we made our way back downstairs.

"Grandma, you better not be in here eating all the crabs," TJ called out to her.

"Oh, shit, y'all got crabs?" I asked, excited.

What better way to get to know my family than over some steamed crabs. I already loved it here.

"When they gone, they gone," Grandma said, cracking a crab open. "Y'all better sit y'all asses down.

"Hey, grandma." I leaned down and kissed her cheek.

"So, you not gonna curse him out for kissing on you? You don't ever let me kiss you." TJ twisted her lips up as we found seats around the table.

"Well, he don't look like he eat no ass." Grandma shook her head from left to right.

I busted out laughing. I wasn't going to out myself.

"I don't be doing that either!" TJ argued, pulling a crab from the box.

"I didn't say you did. I said you look like you did. I can't risk it, baby. You my favorite granddaughter, though." Grandma blew a kiss across the table.

"Y'all wild." I laughed, digging into my crab.

We sat around the table, joking and laughing for a while. The shit felt real, like I wasn't just joining the family. A knock at the door interrupted what we had going on.

"That better not be Pat," Grandma said to TJ but never looked up from the crab in her hand.

"He's our father. Ship should at least know who he is," TJ defended her choice to invite Pat over.

She wiped her hands on a napkin as she got up to answer the door. I wasn't sure how I felt about meeting my father for the first time. In all of my want for a family, I never wished for a better mother. It was never a thought to know my father. I was who I was because of them and in spite of them. They existed even if just in my DNA. It was the people they were attached to that I wanted to know.

I didn't like my mother, but I didn't hate her either. A nigga wasn't out here wondering why she chose drugs over me. Don't nobody choose to be an addict. She had that monkey on her back and couldn't shake it loose. I didn't fuck with her because I didn't like the shit she did.

The only thing I knew about Pat was that he didn't pull out. That wasn't enough to hate him or like him. I knew some triflin' bitches. It was possible that Pat didn't know shit about me. I guess I could be mad at the nigga for being irresponsible. But that's all I had until I heard him out. Pat was at the door, so I didn't have a choice.

Ship

"One thing you're about to learn about Grandma is that she don't do shit she don't want to do. And I'd never ask you to do some shit that I wouldn't do myself," Grandma said, picking out the meat in the crabs.

"I hear you," I responded.

I didn't know what the fuck that meant. I figured it was one of those things that would explain itself. My palms started to sweat as I heard TJ open the door and speak to Pat. I picked through my crab, trying to ignore the sound of their footsteps making their way back into the kitchen. My senses seemed to intensify. I could smell Pat before I saw him. I could feel the hair on my arms. My ears tuned in to the small noises of the house. My thoughts echoed inside my head like it was an empty new apartment. I felt myself disconnecting physically.

"Pat, this is Ship. Ship, this is our father," TJ's voice broke through my disassociation.

"Turn around and let me look at you," Pat's voice boomed through my chest.

That was my first time hearing him speak. I sounded like him. Our tones were the same. The bass that carried when I spoke came from him. I turned around, and my eyes immediately found his.

"Yeah, you one of mine. Who your mama?" Pat asked.

It was like one of those Facebook games or an Instagram

filter that showed what you would look like when you were older. I was looking at the older version of me in real time. The shit was wild as fuck. Scary, too. Pat's hairline was starting to recede. I always feared that. It's why I rarely wore hats. He hadn't started to bald yet, so I guess I had that to look forward to. He looked healthy. Clear skin, no wrinkles. If I saw him on the street, I'd know he was an old nigga getting bitches.

"Na—," I started to speak but the shit came out so slow, I could barely hear myself. A nigga sounded like a scared little boy. I cleared my throat before trying again. "Nadine," I answered.

I looked at the rest of him. He had a beer belly like he was a soccer dad. His facial hair was full, greys hadn't taken over yet. His clothes were fairly new. Pat wore a pair of fresh Air Force Ones. His nails were clean, and the watch on his wrist was expensive.

"Mmhmm," he moaned, nodding his head as he looked me over. "You mine. Nice to meet you." He extended his hand for dap.

My hands were filthy from the crabs. I offered a tap of my forearm instead. Didn't bother to stand for the nigga. I went back to eating my crabs, feeling some type of way. I hadn't been prepared to expect something from him once I saw there wasn't shit wrong with him. Grateful to not have another addict for a parent, I wanted to know why the fuck he wasn't there. He seemed to have his life in order.

"Hey, mama. How you doing?" Pat said to Grandma.

She acted like he wasn't there, tossing the remaining shell of the crab before going for another one. What she had said earlier now made sense. She didn't talk to this nigga. She was telling me that I didn't have to either.

"What's your real name?" Pat asked me as he took a seat across from me.

“Same as yours, I guess,” I said lowly.

“That bitch,” Pat mumbled.

“Pat, that’s still his mama. You don’t know what kind of relationship he got with her. Be respectful,” TJ told him.

“I know what kind of woman she is, and she’s a bitch. I don’t care what he thinks about her. I know her,” Pat defended his choice of words. “I bet he don’t like her ass either.”

Even if I loved my mama, the bitch word ain’t bother me like that. I used it every day. It was my favorite curse word. It could be so many things, and it flowed off my tongue eloquently. Whatever beef Pat and Nadine had was between them. Nadine might be calling Pat bitches, too, if she was ever around for me to ask.

“We don’t have one,” I said aloud. “He can call her whatever he wants. The nigga knows her better than I do.”

An awkward tension filled the room. I don’t know if everyone felt sorry for me, or if it was me calling Pat “nigga”. Something changed.

“I ain’t gon’ hold you,” Pat started to speak. “Ya mama needed some money. I made her exchange the pussy for some cash.”

“He was fucking that girl on the regular,” Grandma spoke, twisting her lips up at me. “She was in my house more than he was. He’d be out running the streets, and she’d be standing in the doorway of my kitchen, scared to ask for some food.”

“But when I met her, it was ‘cause she needed some fucking cash,” Pat argued. “She was trying to get away from her father, or uncle, or something like that. All I know is her peoples weren’t treating her right. It was a bad night at home for her. She wanted some money to stay in a hotel room for the night. I figured I could fuck on her when I wanted. And she could have some place safe to sleep. She was never my woman, though," Pat defended his earlier stance.

"My mama is right about me being gone a lot. I was in the streets. You look like you know what that shit is like." Pat looked to me for confirmation, and I nodded my head. "I'd be outside for days at a time. Grab some fresh clothes from the store and then be out of town living it up and shit."

I laughed at the similarities in my life. That was me and my brothers. Niggas just would up and be out of town like it was nothing. A random trip to Virginia Beach one weekend was how Kiss met Cambria. Crazy how a nigga ain't know shit about Pat but still managed to move through life like him in some ways.

"Few weeks later, she was telling me that she was pregnant. It wasn't hard to tell because the bitch was skinny as a twig. That lil' baby bump looked like a watermelon on her tiny ass." Pat laughed.

I cracked a smile. There was never anyone around to tell me stories about Nadine. Kiss and Kong's mama's prolly knew shit, bad shit that they didn't want to share with me. I never asked them questions about her either. I didn't think I cared. But as I was hearing new news, it was nice to hear the parts of my story that I wasn't there to experience.

"I ain't tryna be an asshole when I say this, but I told her to get an abortion. Put the money in her hand. I drove her to the clinic. She went in and stayed for a while then came back out like she'd gone through with it. I brought her back here to mama's so she could rest. I came home later that week, and she was gone. I figured she realized I didn't love her ass and wanted to get away from me." Pat shrugged. "A part of me did consider that she hadn't gotten the abortion but again, I took her to the clinic and waited for her," Pat explained.

"My son is a liar," Grandma spoke up. "I don't know what part of that is true and what ain't. What I do know, is there's a lie in there somewhere. But even if you choose to believe everything the nigga says, you got to know he ain't shit. Motherfucker tells on himself every time. He figured he could just fuck on ya mama and leave her in my house." Grandma paused from her crabs to count Pat's violations with her fingers. "He told her to get an abortion after saying fucking on her was the plan. The bitch wants a cookie because he took her to the clinic, but did you hear him?" she asked me before continuing. "He waited for her outside. Then dropped her off here and ain't come back for days. The nigga ain't shit!" Grandma yelled at me, but I didn't take offense.

I knew that was for Pat to hear. It didn't matter that Grandma pointed it out to me. I was already in my head, counting his violations. I didn't need her to tell me he wasn't shit. He told me.

"Just like daddy," Pat spat at Grandma. "That's why you hate me so much. Daddy died before you got your nerves up to say that shit to him. I can be all the liars you want, mama, but I remember. I am just like him. I got the shit from somewhere.

TJ stood from the table before Grandma could respond. I personally wanted to hear what Grandma was going to say back.

"I didn't ask Pat here, so you could go in on him like you always do. I just thought my brother might want to hear how he got in this world. That's all. Put a face to the paternal side of his parents. I only wanted Ship to get some of the answers to the questions I had before meeting Pat myself."

"You have an incoming call from Lyin Ass Bitch," Siri alerted in my ear. "Would you like to answer? Say yes or no," Siri instructed.

"Yes," I answered, standing from the table. "My baby mother calling, I gotta take this." I went out to the living room. "Hello?" I answered when the call connected.

"I need you to bring Rhea some sinus medicine. I ran out, and she's going through it right now," Peaches said into the phone.

"Why is you playing?" I asked her. "You can't go to the store? The shit is up the fucking block. I'm busy right now," I told her.

"Ain't nobody playing with my daughter's health. I'm not trying to take her outside and make the shit worse. You too busy, cool. I'll ask her father to do it for her." Peaches hung up in my ear.

That father shit got under my fucking skin, and that bitch knew it, too. A nigga finally moving all the way on and never looking back. Everything going right, and this bitch somehow got the upper hand again. I don't know what I did to piss God off, but he was not allowing Peaches to take this rope from around my neck. A nigga felt like her little puppet. I hated her ass.

Peaches

I went into panic mode when Ship called, telling me that he had a bitch. Instantly, I started crying. My throat burned so bad, I was hoarse the next day. I hoped it was just some shit he said to make a bitch he was trying to fuck happy. In the back of my head, I knew that wasn't the case. Ship never had to try hard for pussy—especially not after being on *Pretty Robots*. That's the reason I got back with him in the first place. I knew bitches would be throwing their pussy left and right in his DM. I had the overwhelming feeling to do something.

It was the same feeling I had after that call. He came to see Rhea the day after, and I could see that bitch all over him. Ship was happy, like on the inside. Some shit not even an argument could take from him. I couldn't even remember him ever being that happy with me, though I'm sure that was just my fear playing tricks on me.

If the bitch he was seeing had made him call me in the middle of the night to set shit straight, he had to be really feeling her ass. It was only a matter of time before he loved her so much that he would stop doing for Rhea. Shit, that girl would be pregnant soon. She'd be giving birth to his real child. I couldn't decide if I'd be madder if she gave him his first son or a daughter that would take my baby's place.

Fresh was clear about wanting nothing to do with Rhea. Ship was the only father she had. Yeah, I could go out and get a new nigga. But he would never love my baby the way Ship did. So, I did the only thing I could. I let Ship think that Fresh was still coming around. Whenever I needed something or even if I didn't, I threatened that I'd get Rhea's real daddy to do it. It's fucked up, but what else was I supposed to do?

If he didn't want to be with me, cool. I fucked shit up with him. But Rhea shouldn't have to pay for my mistakes. I wouldn't allow him to just step out of her life, father or not. Fuck that.

When Ship pulled up, I hurried to rush Rhea up from her sleep. I told her that her daddy was here, and she rushed to the front door. Half sleep, she watched him walk up.

"Daddy baby don't feel good?" Ship stepped in and immediately scooped Rhea up in his arms. Rhea rested her head against his chest, pouting.

Ship thought it was Rhea's allergies that had her looking so out of it. Rhea's been having allergy issues for years. We never ran out of medicine for it. Ship was just so ready to compete with her imaginary father that he'd run over here for anything. He had no idea that I'd simply woken her out of her sleep. She felt warm because she was tucked tightly under the covers. I turned the air off to make her sweat a little.

He sat down in the recliner with her on his lap. Ship started opening the medicine, and I hurried to grab it from him.

"She just had the last of it. I needed it for first thing in the morning," I told him.

Ship twisted his lips up at me, shaking his head. Still, he sat there.

"Daddy, you had crabs?" she said, sniffing his lips.

"I did," he told her.

"Without me?" She lifted her head from his chest.

"I'll bring you some next time," he assured her.

"But I want some now," she whined.

Ship looked down at his watch.

"I can go grab some real quick since you're here with her. I know you said you were busy, but I can just grab a dozen or something like that," I offered.

"Please, daddy?" Rhea poked her lip out.

"Ard." Ship pulled his wallet out and handed me some cash.

"Be right back."

At the door, I slid into my flip flops and rushed out of the house. Rhea wasn't going back to sleep for a while. Since Ship was there, she was going to want him to put her to sleep. So, whatever plans he had were down the fucking drain. I hope that bitch got so mad at him that she cut his ass off.

I walked into the crab spot and placed my order.

"Can I get two dozen medium females?" I asked the cashier.

"That'll be seventy-six dollars."

"That's cool, but can I pay for each dozen separately? Me and my boyfriend are going half, and I don't wanna mix the change up," I told her.

"I got you." She smiled.

I told Ship a dozen but the more crabs I got, the longer he'd have to sit there and pick through them for Rhea. This was chess not checkers.

While waiting for my order, I scrolled IG. I'd been checking Ship's page to see if I could find this new girlfriend of his in his likes or comments. But he rarely fucking posted. He was probably one of those niggas that only had social media to look at half naked bitches. If I couldn't find her ass, I'd make it easy for her to find me.

When I got back to the house, Rhea had Ship helping her

with a puzzle. I quickly snapped a pic from the screen door. My phone was full of cute daddy- daughter moments of them.

“That don’t look like no dozen.” Ship eyed me.

“They were buy one dozen, get a dozen free,” I lied, getting the table ready.

“Where my change?” he asked me, getting up off the floor to help me.

“That’s crazy. A nigga get a girlfriend and now he want his change and shit.” I laughed as I shook my head.

“No, a nigga not with you no more, and I want my change back,” Ship argued.

“Here, boy.” I passed him his twelve dollars.

Rhea stood, holding tight to his leg as Ship spread the last of the sales paper across the table. I took the opportunity to snap another picture. Ship and Rhea dug in. I grabbed a wine cooler from the fridge and turned on some music. With my drink perfectly placed on the table and Ship picking through Rhea’s crabs for her, I took a video of them.

“They good, Rhea?” I asked her from behind the camera.

“They so good, mommy.” Rhea cheesed.

“It’s not a picture, it’s a video, baby,” I told her.

“Oh.” She threw the peace sign up. “This my daddy.” Rhea grabbed his beard.

“Yeah, and daddy thinks you old enough to pick through ya own crabs.” Ship eyed her.

“But I might cut myself, daddy.” She brought her eyebrows together, chewing with her mouth wide open. “I like the way you do it, daddy.”

She made Ship bust out laughing. He kissed her forehead

and fed her some more crab meat. I ended the video, knowing it was the perfect moment. I shared that and the two other pictures to my IG and Facebook and tagged his ass in both. He loved showing off his relationship with Rhea, so he wouldn't care about me tagging him in it.

I doubt he would think it was for malicious reasons. Even when Ship thought the worst of me, he still loved Rhea more than that. Whoever his knew bitch was would have a problem with it—especially if he was supposed to be with her tonight. It was only a matter of time before she made him and Rhea about me and him, and Ship got rid of her ass.

Nevada

"This new little boyfriend of yours is certainly not making the best first impression," my mother said, digging into her salad.

We were supposed to wait for Ship to get here before we started eating. My stepfather got tired of waiting on him. I knew we should have just ridden together, but I got my window fixed on my car and wanted to drive myself.

"He said he's on his way already. He'll be here soon," I assured her.

I was defending him because I felt like I had to. Truth was, I was pissed. It was embarrassing. I talked highly of him, preparing my parents for his arrival, and he didn't have the courtesy to show up on time. I appreciated that he warned me he would be late, but that didn't make me feel any better. If anything, it instantly made me worried. This was only the second man they were meeting, and he was already checking off the ain't shit boxes in their heads.

While they ate, I scrolled IG to pass the time. My salad was getting warm and so was his. I asked my mama to not set his plate until he got here. My father got pissed off, suggesting that I called my mama the help. I hated how he twisted my words, but I loved how he loved my mama. So, I couldn't even be upset about it. One day, Ship would be having the same conversation with our kids in my defense.

Coming across a video of Ship and who I assumed to be

Rhea, I put in one of my Air Pods.

"Nevada, it's rude to have your Air Pods in at the table," my mother said.

I quickly stood from the table and went to the couch. There was no way I was going to miss what was being said in the background. His baby mother took this video. I didn't need proof to know that. I watched the cutest moment of Ship and his daughter and had to love it. She was baiting me. It was just woman's intuition.

I clicked on her profile, and it was public. She was cute. A hood rat ass bitch but cute still. She definitely didn't have shit on me but her daughter. And that was only until I was pregnant, if I wasn't already. If this bitch wanted to know who I was, she could. Only one of us would be crying ourselves to sleep, and it wouldn't be me. I went back to Ship's page and left the heart made out of hands emoji under the pic of Rhea holding tight to his leg. I was pissed that this was the reason he was late, but it wasn't enough to make me bow out. It was clear that Ship's new bitch had her ass shook. I wasn't going anywhere. Let the petty wars begin.

A knock at the door let me know Ship was here. I stuffed my Air Pod back into the case and answered the door.

"What's up?" He leaned in, giving me a hug and a kiss on the cheek. "My bad about being late," he apologized.

"It's my parents you need to apologize to," I mumbled as I shut the door behind him.

"Mommy and dad, this is Patrick. Patrick, this is my mother, Delores, and my stepdad, Grant." I stood at the table, making introductions. "You can sit right here." I tapped the chair next to mine as I took my seat.

"Nice to meet y'all. I'm sorry I'm late. I was with my daughter. I did stop and grab these gas cards, though." Ship pulled two gas cards from his pocket with twenty-five dollars a piece on them.

"Now in the movies, the little boy trying to date your daughter brings flowers, but I like this." My mother smiled.

"You alright with me," my dad said, shoving the card in his pocket.

That was a nice gesture, smart, too. But he was going to need more than a gas card to make this shit up to me. I'm thinking he can eat me until I cry.

"So, you say you have a daughter," my mother started. "How old is she?"

Ship answered those questions and all her others. I don't know how Ship felt about all of this, but it felt like an interview to me. It was uncomfortable watching him be drilled. Ultimately, he could say anything to them and do the opposite. I never understood why this was necessary. My dad didn't say much of anything until the end of the dinner.

"You know, I've watched you answer all of my wife's questions. I think you have a good head on your shoulders. You sound like a wonderful father. It doesn't seem to me that you're trying to get over. So, I don't have any questions. But I do have something to say before you leave."

"Thank you, sir. I pride myself on being a good father," Ship responded.

"All I ask is that you do not put hands on her, and you don't leave her stranded anywhere. Y'all gon' go through your shit but as long as you take care of her in your anger and frustrations, we good." My father held out his hand for Ship to shake.

"Yes, sir. I got her," Ship assured him.

"I believe you do. Have a good night," my dad said.

"It was a pleasure meeting you." My mother leaned in for a hug.

"It was nice meeting you, too. Y'all have a good night as well," Ship said as we left.

"Thank you, mommy." I gave her a tight squeeze.

"Oh, you're welcome, baby. He handled himself well. I can't say that I like him yet, but I don't hate him," she said.

"You know your mama likes to play tough. I think he's a fine young man." My dad gave me a hug.

"Thank you, dad," I told him. "See y'all."

I walked down the steps to meet Ship on the sidewalk.

"I'm sorry for being late," Ship said before I could get a complaint out.

"Why were you late?" I asked him as he walked me to my car.

I already knew the answer, but I wanted to see if he would tell me the truth. He hadn't pulled his phone out all night. He didn't see that I already saw what he was doing. It was the perfect opportunity to lie to me.

"Peaches said Rhea needed some medicine. She got real bad allergies, so I went to grab it. When I got there, Rhea smelled I had crabs, and she wanted some. Then she ain't want me to leave until she fell asleep. I swear, I wanted to be here on time. I promise that tonight is not a reflection of how I feel about you, nor is it a reflection on how I prioritize you. I'm in this. I got both feet in, all eggs in your basket. I'm for real ," he said, pulling me into him for a hug.

"I believe you. This is an adjustment for the both of us. I'd like to think we are both doing the best we can."

"I swear I am." Ship kissed me. "This shit moving fast. And

I don't want it to slow down. It's just taking me a minute to catch up," he assured me. "But it's been a long ass day. I'm tryna jump in the shower, maybe eat you in the shower." He kissed on me some more. "And put you in a headlock until we fall asleep." Ship laughed.

"You gotta relax with that." I laughed. "Be having me choking in my sleep and shit. Where you think I'm going?" I asked him.

"Nowhere. I just be wanting to be as close to you as possible." After one last kiss, Ship opened my door. "Beat you to the house," he said before shutting me in my car.

I sped off before he could get in his car. It was hard to stay mad at his ass. One minute, I'm ready to read his ass for filth. The next, I'm craving to cum on his dick. I often replayed our conversations back in my head. We communicated well. I was letting shit slide because he was apologizing. And not just that; he understood what he was apologizing for. Even in his moments of frustration with me, he talked to me like he had some sense. Why would I hold on to the bullshit when he was actively trying to get it right?

Somehow, Ship made it to my apartment before I did. He got out of his car when he saw me pull up. Opening my door and helping me out of the car, he tongued me down against the car.

"I don't think that apology was good enough," he said. "I need to put some action behind it."

"I feel you, but can we do it in the house?" I laughed.

"What's the point? They be hearing you screaming all night. They might as well get to see it, too," he said.

We bust out laughing as I punched him in his arm. I grabbed his hand, leading the way up the steps.

"Well, tonight, this apology better make me scream out

your government."

"Nah. I'ma make you name our kids." He tapped my ass as we walked in the house.

Ship tried to get some shower sex started, but I wasn't with it. Fucking in the shower was never my thing. I hated fighting over the water. And as freaky as I was in the bedroom, a bitch didn't like uncomfortable positions. I needed to be on a sturdy surface. I was never the girl trying to get fucked upside down against the wall. While Ship was in the shower, I pulled my rose from my nightstand. I found me some lesbian porn and started our session without him.

While I wasn't into bitches, watching them in porn turned me on. They were so into one another. It was passionate and feral. And they could cum over and over. My pussy always pulsated at the sound of a woman giving out instructions for the other girl to follow. She was keeping that bitch in line, and that's what made me leak through the sheets every time.

Ship walking into the bedroom, wiping his face with the towel sent me up a notch.

"Oh, shit." I snatched the rose from my clit. "Eat my cum, baby."

He never hesitated to please me. Ship quickly rushed his head between my legs, and I squirted in his face. This nigga kept sucking my clit. This is why I wasn't coming up off this nigga.

"Do that shit again," he said.

I put the rose back on my clit, and Ship slid his dick inside of me. The combo sent chills through my body.

"Harder, baby harder," I urged him.

Ship pounded into me until I felt my juices building up. I tried to push him out of me so I could let it all out, but he wouldn't budge. My juices went all over his chest as Ship stared me in my eyes.

"Do that shit again," he ordered me.

I was getting off from the fact that he thought I was the sexiest bitch in the world right now. He wanted to see my pussy make art all over him. Pleasing me was getting him where he needed to be. I loved that for me.

Nevada

I thought I woke up to take a quick piss. On the way out of my bathroom, I heard knocking at my door. That must have been what woke me out my sleep. In my pajamas, I went to the door.

"Who is it?" I called out when I was close enough to hear a response.

"Jemari," my baby father said on the other side of the door.

I already talked to him about Ship. He said he didn't have an issue with it because he didn't want me anymore. That could have all been a lie just to get me to let my guard down. I was scared as fuck to open the door.

"Girl, what the fuck is you doing? Open the fucking door," Jemari barked on the other side.

I rushed to open the door before Ship woke up from all the yelling Jemari was doing in the hallway.

"What's up?" I snatched the door open.

"Damn, a nigga been gone for almost a year, and that's all I get?" he asked.

"Welcome home." I scrunched my face up. "What you want?"

"Girl, stop playing with me." Jemari walked in the house. "I came to see my son. Mari!" Jemari called out.

"He's at your mama's house," I told him. "So, you can go see him over there."

I tried to usher him out of the front door. My bedroom door opened, making Jemari turn around. Ship walked towards us up the hallway. My stomach turned in knots, not knowing what the fuck was about to happen.

"Ship, this is my son's father, Jemari. Jemari, this is my boyfriend, Ship," I introduced them, not knowing what else to do.

"What's up?" Ship nodded his head towards Jamari as he stepped into the kitchen.

"What's good?" Jemari tossed a nod back at Ship.

Ship grabbed a water from the fridge and guzzled damn near the whole bottle.

"Baby, I'm hungry," he told me. "You wanna go out?" he asked me.

"Yeah, that's cool," I responded.

"Come get dressed," he said as he walked out of the kitchen.

"I'm coming," I assured him as he closed my bedroom door.

"Let me get out of here before you get in trouble with your man. He looks like he don't play with your ass. I like that. Maybe he can buy your ass a muzzle for that big ass mouth of yours." Jemari laughed as he walked out of the front door.

"Shut the fuck up," I spat before shutting and locking the door.

I didn't expect that shit to go so smoothly. Ship walking out of my bedroom like the place was his could have gone left. I guess Jemari was really over my ass. Now if Peaches could get over Ship, we'd be getting somewhere.

At breakfast, Ship and I sat beside each other, waiting on our food. My father called me just as the waitress was dropping our plates off.

"Hi, daddy." I cheesed into the screen like the daddy's girl I was.

"Baby girl, what you doing?"

"At breakfast with my boyfriend."

Instincts made me show Ship's face. I cringed on the inside. That was the last part of my family that Ship hadn't met yet. This was not the proper introduction.

"How you doing?" Ship asked, wiping his mouth with a napkin.

"I'm good and you?" My daddy asked him.

"I'm doing good."

"Nevada is going to have to schedule something so we can meet," Daddy said.

"Just tell me the time and the place, sir." Ship nodded his head.

"Ok, daddy." I put the camera back on my face. "I'll text you when we're free. I'm about to dig into my food."

"Ard, don't forget." He twisted his lips up before ending the call.

"Sorry about that. I don't know why I did that," I explained myself.

"It's cool. I ain't tripping. I done met everybody else already." Ship laughed.

I laughed but it quickly faded when I realized I had only met TJ, his grandma, and Kiss. He said he had another brother and their people. Why hadn't he introduced me to anyone yet?

"When am I going to start meeting your people?" I asked, cutting into my pancakes.

"What you doing today?" he asked me.

"I have to pick Jemari up from his grandma's house tonight. It's the last week of school," I told him. "But that's not till later."

"Then today. You can meet my other brother and his bitch. Technically, you already met him. But we can do it the right way. His mama and his sisters might be around." Ship drank his orange juice.

"That simple?" I asked him.

"That simple." He nodded.

Shit with him was so easy. I asked and he delivered. A bitch could get used to all of this. When we left Denny's, Ship said we were going to meet his brother, Kong. He gave me this really detailed speech as we parked in from of his house.

"These motherfuckers crazy. Like not for play, play. His bitch had a hit out on him at one point."

"Huh?" I asked, scrunching my face in disbelief.

"Exactly. Don't look at her too long, or him. They both paranoid as a motherfucker, thinking somebody is coming for payback from their pasts. These niggas might get to fighting. If Wynter is here, just avoid her ass at all costs, because she likes to fight. Whilemena is going to asks questions that ain't none of her business. And Whit is autistic. His mama is like my mama, so when we get back in this car, don't be asking me what's wrong with certain motherfuckers." He eyed me as we got out of the car.

He was referring to when I asked him what was wrong with Kiss. Ship hadn't let that shit go yet. The excitement of meeting someone in Ship's circle had left. Now I was stuck, trying to remember all the rules he gave me for what not to do.

At the basement door, I could hear somebody growling.

"Oh, my Gah," I whispered, with my mouth open.

"See," Ship said to me as he opened the door.

The shit wasn't even locked. He walked right in like he lived here. And my goofy ass was right behind him.

"Fuck y'all got going on?" Ship asked, dapping Kong up. I remembered him from the barbershop.

"Schetta fucking playing with me."

"Kong, ain't nobody playing with you. I was with my aunties. I told your ass that already. Hey, bro." Schetta gave Ship a hug and a kiss like she wasn't cursing Kong out.

"This my girl, Nevada. Nevada, this my brother, Kong. Y'all already met. This his girl, Schetta."

"Hey." Schetta smiled at me.

"'Sup," Kong nodded his head before turning back to Schetta. "But what the fuck you doing over there? Keep leaving me in the house with the damn baby. Like, stop fucking playing with me."

"None of your fucking business," Schetta responded far less animated. It was almost as if she was unbothered by Kong's theatrical ass.

"I bet the next time you leave out this motherfucker, I'm going with you," Kong threatened.

Ship nodded his head towards the steps to follow him. He didn't have to ask twice. The argument Kong and Schetta were having was none of my business. Upstairs, a light-skinned girl ran behind a toddler.

"Whit, what's up?" Ship interrupted their running and grabbed the little boy up.

"Hi, Patrick." Whit waved. "Who this?" She smiled at me.

"Whit, that's my girlfriend. Her name is Nevada. Nevada,

this is my sister, Whit," Ship introduced us.

"Hi." I waved at her.

"Hi." She waved back.

"When you gon' get out these diapers, boy?" Ship played with the toddler.

He giggled himself into a laughing fit.

"Saint, this Uncle P girlfriend. Her name Nevada. You gon' say hi?"

"What's up?" The little boy gave me a head nod.

I busted into laughter because I ain't ever seen no shit like that. It was obvious he was his father's son.

"Hi." I went to tickle him, and he moved backwards in Ship's arm.

"Don't touch me," he said before turning his head.

"Oop," I pursed my lips.

"Stop being a bad ass," Ship told him before putting him on the floor.

"Aye, Ship. Where ya Vegas girl at?" Kong's voice got closer as he walked up the steps.

"Right here. And she ain't from Vegas. Her name is Nevada," Ship corrected him.

"My bad. Check this shit. Schetta been going over her auntie's 'cause they been tryna talk her into carrying a baby," Kong explained.

Ain't no way this was any of our business. Especially not mine. Like, we were talking about Schetta's pussy basically. They didn't even know me. This shit was wild. I was going to chime in since they were asking, though.

"Well, can her auntie and uncle not have kids on their own?" I asked.

"They're lesbians," Schetta said, laughing as she appeared from the basement.

"Oh." I pursed my lips.

"This all I'm saying," Kong started again. "If she gonna carry their baby, she can go over to one of them little centers that pay big money for that shit. Fuck that."

"It's my aunt, nigga. They do everything for me." Schetta rolled her eyes at him.

"Then what the fuck do I do?" Kong put his hands to his chest. "I guess I can quit working then, and you can take care of us." Kong threw his arms up dramatically.

Kong was entertaining, but I'd be lying if I said I would deal with his ass. He was too much. There could only be one dramatic person in the relationship. And it was me. Always gonna be me. Kong and Kiss seemed to be the opposite extremes. Kiss was quiet, calm, and collected while Kong was rowdy, wild, and loud. My baby must have been somewhere in the middle.

"You know that's not what I meant. At the end of the day, it's my body, my auntie, and my decision." Schetta moved around the kitchen.

"You right about one thing. Those ain't my aunties. But that's my body," he pointed with his fingers, "and those my eggs. If you gonna let another nigga fertilize one of *my* eggs and carry somebody else's baby in *my* body for nine months, I'm getting a cut," Kong said, grabbing his dick like it was a weapon. "Straight up."

"Ain't no ring on my finger." Schetta put her hand in the light like she was checking a hundred-dollar bill.

"And ain't gon' be one either, if you don't start acting right around this motherfucker."

Kong and Ship bust out laughing while me and Schetta looked at them like they were crazy.

"You done had enough fun," I told Ship. "Time to go."

"Nah, you wanted to meet these motherfuckers, right?" Ship laughed. "When I'ma meet your peoples?" Ship mocked me.

I was so embarrassed. My mouth dropped and I could feel my chest tighten and my cheeks warm.

"She embarrassed," Kong said, laughing harder. His phone rang.

Ship tried to kiss and hug on me for putting me out there. I wasn't letting him kiss on me at all.

"Damn, yo." Kong stood with a straight face. "That's fucked up."

Kong's eyes watered. Ship got serious. I could see the fear on his face. He didn't even know what happened, but his brother was hurting, so he was hurting.

"Yeah, hit me when you on the way in the house. I'ma call Ship, don't worry about it. We be over there," Kong said, eyeing Ship as he hung up the phone.

"Bitch, what's wrong? Fuck is you playing guessing games for? Rip the fucking Band-Aid off," Ship pleaded with him.

"Kiss mom got cancer," Kong said.

I rushed to Ship while Schetta rushed to Kong. The both of us rubbed their backs while they wore the distraught faces of men who'd been to war and were returning home to find out they'd lost what they thought was back at home, waiting for them. I felt so bad for my baby.

It was selfish, but I got another glimpse into the things

Ship cared about. How would me and my son fit?

Peaches

That bitch played right into my hand. Ion think that hoe waited a whole hour before she was commenting on my baby's pictures. I can't lie. It took me a minute to find her ass because there were so many bitches in Ship's comments since that *Pretty Robots* bullshit, but I knew it was her when I clicked on her shit. She hadn't come out and outright posted Ship on her page yet. She posted little shit, though. A piece of his shoulder or his beard. Shit that I knew like the back of my hand.

Scrolling her page, I found out she had a son, a good relationship with her baby father that I recognized from high school, and support. Even if I erased Ship from this picture, I was still jealous of her. All I had was Ship. No one else was watching my kid for me. If Rhea needed to go to the emergency room, me or Ship would have to take her. If I wanted to do something with my life, I'd be disqualified for food stamps, housing, and anything else that I needed.

I was stuck in this bullshit ass cycle. Without Ship, I wouldn't be able to do the little that I do for Rhea. She thinks crabs here and there is everything. She loves having all kinds of snacks in the pantry. But that's because she was five. Soon, my baby would be a big girl, and I'd never be able to do enough. I needed Ship. Rhea needed Ship. desert bitch was going to have to make do with what she already had. She couldn't have him.

"Ahhh!" I dropped my phone onto the carpet. "No, no, no, no, no, no." I picked it up, as if the screen might have broken. I knew it wasn't. I did the worst shit possible. I hit follow on

Desert bitch's page. There was no point in unfollowing her; she would get the notification anyhow.

"Mommy, can you call my daddy?" Rhea played with the beads in her hair.

"No, but you can."

"Thank you."

Rhea leaned against the couch, with her legs crossed at the ankles. I dialed Ship's number and passed her the phone.

"Daddy," Rhea sighed into the phone. "Can you come over here and read my book to me?" She rolled her eyes up in her head. "But mommy don't read like you do."

"Excuse me?" I interrupted.

"Shh." Rhea put her hand up to me. "I'm tryna talk to my Daddy."

"Girl, ard, now. You doing too much. I'll hang that motherfucking phone up," I snapped on her ass.

Rhea burst into tears. "She yelling at me," she managed to get out clear as day. "Ok." Rhea nodded her head, passing me my phone back.

She took off, running for her room.

"Hello?" I answered the phone.

"Aye, can you get her bathed and ready for bed? I'ma come read her a book, but I got something to do, Peaches. I can't be late. I need her ass to roll over and go to sleep," Ship asked.

"She's already had a bath. I'll rub her down in some of that melatonin lotion, though. And I know how to fucking read. You don't have to come over here. She just being a spoiled brat," I offered, knowing that's not what I wanted. Ship wasn't going for it anyhow.

"Man, just have her ready for bed, please."

"Nigga, I said ard. Don't piss me off," I snapped on him before hanging up in his ear.

That showing off shit got me hot. Ship was on my case about stupid shit like what she wore but never corrected that smart ass mouth of hers. He thought that shit was funny. I had something funny for his ass.

"Rhea, come here!" I called out to her as I walked into the kitchen.

"Yes," Rhea pouted.

"Here." I passed her a Little Debbie zebra cake. "Mommy is sorry for making you cry. Ok?"

"I forgive you," she said.

"You can't tell daddy about this snack, ok? You know he don't like you eating snacks before bed," I warned her against ratting on me.

"I won't." She stuck out her pinky finger.

We made a pinky promise that she wouldn't say anything. When she did that, she would for sure keep her word. I didn't care who her real daddy was, she got that secret keeping from me and Ship. Although, Fresh was a lying ass nigga, too. My baby got it honest.

When she finished that cake, I washed her face and rubbed her down with that lotion just so Ship would smell it. His ass was in for a rude awakening.

"Daddy!" Rhea ran out to the living room when she heard Ship pull up.

His music rattled the windows. She stared out of the blinds.

"Get out my blinds!" I told her.

Rhea left the window and opened the door. She put her tiny fingers on the screen door. I loved how excited she got about him. There was no opportunity for me to get that reaction from her. I was always in the house.

I hadn't gone out with my girls since Ship moved out. And even when I did, Rhea was either sleep when I got back or just content with her daddy, that she didn't care about me. I know my baby loved me, but Ship was her favorite person.

My throat burned, thinking about what I did to her. Like, how dare Ship not be her father. She deserved him. He deserved the love she gave him. She was the only person in the world to give it to him. I don't know what any of us would do if we weren't a family anymore.

I hurried to wipe the tears that were building as Ship walked through the door. Rhea extended her arms out to him. I watched him pick her up and hold her tightly like he desperately needed to see her instead of the other way around. He didn't have that glow that he'd been sporting. Maybe him and desert bitch broke up.

"Hey," I said.

"What's up? I'm gonna go read to her till she falls asleep," Ship said, walking past me.

"Ok." I nodded my head.

Rhea wasn't going to be sleep no time soon. I didn't know what was going on, but I was kicking him while he was down.

"Wait." I jumped out, catching him at the top of the hallway.

In the kitchen, I grabbed the melatonin from the top of the fridge. Pulling one from the plastic jar, I passed it to him. Rhea chewed the gummy, and they disappeared down the hall into her bedroom. I was back on the couch, feet bent at the knees, watching TV. My phone chimed with a notification.

Desert bitch followed me back. I guess she and Ship weren't broken up. Was this bitch trying to be my friend? Or was she joining in on the game I was playing? I wasn't sure, but I wasn't trying to be her friend. I didn't want her around Ship, let alone my daughter. If she was just playing the same game I was, I had something for her ass. If they weren't broken up when he got here, they would be by the time he left.

I felt enough time had passed that Rhea should be sleep. I muted the TV to see if I could hear Ship reading. My house was silent. Like maybe his ass had fallen asleep, too. I tiptoed into Rhea's bedroom. She was knocked out like I thought. Ship was sitting on the floor. Rhea's dresser was supporting his back as he stared at her sleeping.

"You ard?" I asked him, stepping further into her room.

Ship didn't respond; he only shook his head. He lifted himself from the ground and dusted his hands on his jeans. I led the way to the living room.

"What's wrong?" I asked with one arm folded across the other.

"Rhea's sperm donor still coming around?" he asked me as he took a seat on the recliner.

"Yeah." I nodded my head, lying. "She just thinks that he's my friend, though. She doesn't know that he's her father."

"He not. I'm her father. You and that nigga can do what y'all want. Get married. Have a football team of kids if you want. But Peaches, Rhea is mine. I'm not tryna hear nothing else. I been here, I'm gone be here. She don't need that nigga for shit," Ship explained.

I had no argument with that. Especially since her father wasn't around and had no plans on coming around. Ship was all

I had; he just didn't know that.

"Ok. But you can't be her father on your time. When I need something, I need something. I shouldn't have to ask twice. I honestly shouldn't have to ask at all. You should be here with us," I said.

It was risky, but I was taking the chance. Ship was going through something. It was fucked up to me to try and play on his vulnerability, but I had no choice.

"Why ain't I here?" he asked me.

The tone of his question was that of a parent reprimanding a child. His sadness hadn't allowed him to go easy on me. I'm guessing Rhea not being his was a part of how he was feeling. It was worth a shot, though.

"For what it's worth, I wish Rhea was yours."

"Yeah, me, too." Ship twisted his lips up at me.

"I don't see why we can't be friends, though, Ship. I didn't cheat on you and make her. I was already pregnant with her when I met you. You treating me like I did some shady shit to you or tricked you for all these years or something. I didn't know. I found out she wasn't yours the same time you found out that she wasn't yours," I tried to reason with him.

"That's bullshit because from the moment Rhea told you I did the test, you started being weird as fuck. It was like you knew already. That's why I was so anxious to get the fuck outta here," he argued. "Let's not leave out the fact the whole reason I got the test was because you hollered out that she wasn't mine.

"I said she wasn't yours to be a smart ass. There was always a possibility that she wasn't, but she's such a mini you that I thought it was slim to none. I pushed that shit to the back of my head. But when I found out about the test, I got scared that I had it wrong all these years. I'm sorry. But we still need you," I spoke through the pain in my throat.

"I got a girl, Peaches. I love her ass. I'm always going to be here for Rhea. If she needs it, I got it. But me moving back in, us getting back together or even fucking, is dead. I don't even wanna touch you, bruh. If it wasn't for Rhea, I'd never talk to your ass again."

Tears fell at the harshness of his words. He wasn't speaking to me like he never cared about me. We had history. He loved me more than I loved him at one point. Now he just didn't give a fuck about me.

"I know that shit hurt to hear. It ain't really a nice way to tell you that I don't fuck with you like that. A nigga still got love for you, though. I'm always gonna have that. But you took something from me, and I'm tired of losing shit. I just found all this family and now I'm losing something again," Ship said.

"Family?" I asked, confused.

"I got a grandma and a sister. Met my pops, too." Ship smiled. "And my girl got all this family."

"And you will always have Rhea. I'll never take her from you. So, what are you losing?" I asked him.

I wanted so bad for the answer to be me. If he showed a little sadness about things being over with us, I don't know. It would make me feel better knowing that he didn't want to go; he just felt like he had to. The easier it was for him to be done with me, the more painful it felt to me. He'd been out of the house for over a year now, but he was still here a lot. It wasn't until he got with the Desert Bitch that he started to fall back.

"Kiss's mom has cancer, and the shit is fucking me up," Ship confessed.

"I'm so sorry to hear that," I gasped.

For years, this was our little family. Me and Ship, Kong,

Tessa and Mont, and Kiss and Cambria. Mont was gone, and Tessa might as well have died with him because she wasn't around. She wasn't letting us around Reagan either. As women, none of us were close but when we were around one another, we had a good time. It wasn't just my household that had changed. All of us had changed. Things seemed to have flipped with the snap of a finger.

Ship and I talked for a good little while. I went to the bathroom and came back out to him dozed off in the recliner. We had such a special moment. Like he was agreeing to a friendship. But I couldn't miss the opportunity to snap a picture of him, over here sleeping, with no Rhea in sight. It was a nice welcome pic for Desert Bitch as my new follower. Ship didn't want to be with me. Okay. But he couldn't be with her either.

Ship

Nevada moved around the room silently while giving sound to everything she touched. I swear I could literally hear her snatching the hair spray up. She sprayed that shit all around her head before slamming it on the bathroom sink. I stood in the doorway, head against the frame, letting her have her attitude.

I fucked up three nights ago, and she hadn't let the shit go yet. I mean, we hadn't even discussed it. Yet, we were on our way to her sister's house for a game night. The one scheduled a few weeks back, we missed. Nevada and Denver hadn't made up at the time, and Nevada chose to sit that one out.

I wasn't feeling this shit when we had so much tension between us. Her real dad was supposed to be here, and it would be my first time meeting him. The initial introduction had been made on the phone last week. I was in the background as Nevada scheduled dinner with her father and stepmom. That's why she was so mad.

I don't know what the fuck happened. Peaches called me over because Rhea was crying for me. I went because I'd been picking up overtime at work with the bros and hadn't seen her in a few days. A nigga was getting off work and passing the fuck out. I missed Rhea as much as she missed me. The plan was to sit with her for two hours then pick Nevada up so we could meet her parents for dinner. A nigga fell asleep over Peaches crib, for real .

Peaches's stupid ass posted a pic of me knocked out on the recliner. Proof that I wasn't in that bitch bed or nothing. Nevada wasn't trying to hear that shit, though. Point was, I missed meeting her other set of parents and I stayed the night at my baby mother's house. I was kind of happy she didn't allow me to explain myself because I ain't have no excuse. I was sleepy and fell asleep.

"Can you move?" Nevada asked, trying to make her way out of the bathroom.

There was more than enough space for her to exit. She was just being a bitch. I moved out of her way anyhow.

"I'm going to the car," I told her, making my way down the steps.

I grabbed my keys and left her in the apartment. This the shit that made a nigga want to be single. I felt like a little kid waiting for his mom to get home and give him an ass whipping. My mama ain't never did that shit but still. It was like I was in trouble. I wished she would speak her peace, so a nigga could at least get that feeling up off me.

Nevada got in the car, making sure to slam my door. She let out a heavy exhale, crossing one arm over the other.

"Where I'm going?" I asked Nevada as I pulled from in front of her place.

"You don't have my sister's address in your phone already? You picked me up from there a few weeks back," she snapped.

I found an open space on the busy street and parked.

"Aye, get that shit off your chest, or I can take you back to the house and take my ass home," I told her.

"And where is home again? The place you have with Kiss or Peaches's place?" Nevada put her finger to her chin and smushed her lips together.

"Stop fucking playing with me. Your house is more home

than her shit. You know that. You mad, I get it. But a nigga ain't fucking on her. I barely speak to the bitch."

"Right, you just stay the fucking night," Nevada mumbled.

"I was on the fucking recliner!" I was yelling now because she was pissing me off. "You saw me on the fucking picture, my nigga. She took the only pic she could get, posted that shit to get under your skin, and you took the fucking bait. A nigga ain't had his shit sucked in three motherfucking days!"

"Oh, boo fucking hoo," Nevada twisted her lips up. "Why you think a bitch wanna suck or fuck anything after you embarrassed me like that? I showed up to dinner with my parents, late, and by my damn self. Fuck out of here."

"I'm sorry, man. It happened already. Ain't shit I can do except go back in time and not fall asleep. And believe you me, if they had a time machine for sale, I would buy one just so you could cut this weird shit the fuck out," I told her. "How long you supposed to not be talking to me for? This the most you said to me since that shit happened. The shit ain't making me want to be around."

"If you don't want to be around, then go the fuck home!" Nevada yelled.

"That's not what a nigga said. I ain't tryna sit around in silence until you decide you done punishing me. I'm not your child. I took accountability for my fuck up. I acknowledged that shit and apologized. Like what you want to hear to move past this shit? 'Cause this ain't working," I told her.

"What you mean by it's not working? You want to break up?" she asked.

Bitches were dumb as fuck sometimes. I'm in the car, on my way to her sister's place to meet her daddy, and she asking me if I want to break up. Bitches wanted you to read their minds and in between the lines but needed you to spell out every fucking thing to them.

"Breaking up is not an option. But neither is you having an attitude for seventy-two fucking hours. So, what you want me to say? What do I gotta do so we can get on the other side of this?" I asked her.

"I want to get over it. I want to let it go. But I feel like your baby mother is playing a game and you're letting her. You feed into it every time. I don't want to let this go just for you to do it again. Like, you can't promise that Peaches won't have you floating across my social media tomorrow," she mumbled.

"That part is on you. Both of y'all playing games with each other. Like why the fuck would y'all follow each other on IG?" I scrunched my face. "You playing her game like y'all in competition. You heard me tell that bitch I was with you. Why you even trippin' off her?" I asked.

I didn't understand it because I wasn't playing games with neither of them. It wasn't a situation where I was trying to have my cake and eat it, too. Both of them knew what it was. Instead of trusting me, she was trusting the illusion Peaches was trying to create on social media.

"You asked what I need you to do," Nevada started. "I want her to stop posting you on her social media. You can post pictures with your daughter. Why does she have to post them? Do that, and the Peaches thing won't be an issue," Nevada said.

"Hey, Siri," I called out, wiping my hands down my face.

"Mmhmm," she answered.

"Call Lyin Ass Bitch," I told her as I rested my head against the headrest.

I couldn't act like I didn't know what the fuck Nevada was talking about. For weeks, Peaches been posting pics of a nigga—different outfits too—like I was still living in the house, and we were still together. Even the bros were clowning me about the shit. Nevada wasn't asking for much. It's a conversation I should have been had with Peaches.

"Hey, Ship. What's up?" Peaches yawned into the phone.

"Aye, look. You gotta stop posting all them pictures of me," I told her straight up.

"So, what you tryna hide our daughter or something?" Peaches asked.

"Please be fucking for real for one damn second. You know what the fuck you doing. You tryna make that shit look like something else. It's causing issues with what I got going on. You want to take the pictures, cool, but send them to me and I'll post them," I offered.

"This shit is not coming from you. You don't even care about social media like that. That desert bitch is in your ear. You want to let her draw a wedge between you and your daughter, so be it." Peaches ended the call.

"Desert bitch?" Nevada asked. "That's how you let that bitch talk about me?" she snapped.

I kept my composure, but that shit was funny as fuck. Desert bitch? Nevada? Bitches were so clever when they were talking their shit.

"It's no different than all the different names you call her. I ignore her ass the same way I ignore you when you do it. I don't care about that shit. It's dumb." I shrugged. "I did what you asked me. She ain't posting no more pictures. You won, if it was some kind of game you got going with her. But I'd like to play some real games. Have a drink or two, meet your daddy, so is we sliding or what?" I asked her. "Because a nigga can go in the house and jump on the game, too." I turned my head in her direction, still leaning against the seat.

"We can go to my sister's," she said plainly.

"That's what a nigga thought," I mumbled.

Nevada mushed the shit out of my head, and I laughed. "Don't fucking push it," she smiled.

"Ard, ard. Keep your hands to your motherfucking self. Sometimes my reflexes respond before I can," I warned her.

Nevada mushed me repeatedly at the stop light. In one smooth motion, I had the back of her neck, and her little ass was helpless.

"See," I shook my head, "a nigga tried to warn you. You want to keep playing. Say you sorry," I told her.

"Hell no." She laughed. "Get off me, Ship, 'fore you mess up my hair," she whined.

As the light turned green, I moved her by her neck to my face, making her kiss me.

"Damn." I let her go, licking my lips. "A nigga ain't taste you in days. That just lifted my motherfucking spirits." I played with her.

"Mine, too," Nevada whispered, massaging the back of my neck.

The rest of the ride, we stayed just like that, singing along to the songs that came through the speaker. This is what a nigga was going to have a hard time letting go off. Her little ass felt like home. It was fucked up that this was probably the best it was going to get until I put a baby in her ass.

Nevada was ready to introduce me to Demari, but I knew Peaches wasn't going for me introducing her to Rhea. And Rhea wasn't my daughter, so a nigga ain't really have no say about it. A baby of our own would force Nevada to look past not meeting Rhea and move on with the parts of our lives outside of that.

That shit ain't happened yet and if it didn't soon, I might lose her ass.

Nevada

Sometimes, I struggled with whether or not I was letting Ship off too easy. Peaches was a real problem in our relationship. That was the second time he called her in my face to do what I asked of him. But, for some reason, it wasn't enough. If I was being honest, I wanted him away from that bitch. Which in turn meant, I wanted him to drop Rhea, too. That was fucked up. I didn't see any other way when Peaches obviously still wanted her family.

It felt like this would never be our family. Especially when we tried non-stop, but these pregnancy tests kept coming up negative. The shit was starting to wear on me because I felt like a baby was the only thing that would hold Ship and me together. He said breaking up wasn't an option, but that was only until one of us pushed the other past their breaking point.

We walked into my sister's house, and the party immediately stopped. All eyes went towards me and Ship.

"Ain't you that boy from *Pretty Robots*?" Vincent's cousin asked.

"He ain't no boy," I snapped. "He a grown ass man and mine. Put your face in your phone or something," I told her.

"Hey, baby girl." My daddy stretched his arms out to me for a hug while the house went back to whatever game they were playing.

"Hi, daddy." I let him squeeze me tightly. "This is my boyfriend, Patrick. Baby, this is my daddy, Lenox. And that's my stepmother, Michelle," I introduced them as I gave my stepmom a hug.

"Nice to meet you." My father and Ship dapped.

"Where the drinks at?" I asked, grabbing my stepmom's arm, leaving Ship with my daddy.

They walked past us and out the back door. They were probably going to smoke one. My daddy was out the streets, but he loved his weed.

"Now why you come in here, snapping on your sister's friend? You know how that girl is about her friends." Michelle raised her eyebrows at me.

"Oh, please. That's not her friend. That's Vince's cousin. Every time Denver and her bum get into it, that girl be all over social media, talking big shit about Denver. Fuck that girl," I said, taking a shot.

I don't care if me and my sister argue every day, I would still beat a bitch ass about her. Denver was the definition of forgive and forget. While me, I rested on the beautiful line of giving a bitch hell until she learned her lesson.

"I done told that girl to stop telling us everything and expecting us to be as forgiving as her. This motherfucker could be on fire, and I'd grab you girls and lock the door on their asses," Michelle said.

The two of us burst into laughter, interrupting the entire party. There were two separate games going on, along with music blasting. How I kept putting a halt to shit, had me feeling uneasy. It's like everybody in this motherfucker was waiting for something to pop off with me. I hadn't planned to whip no ass, but that could change at any minute.

I threw another shot back, watching the room as they were watching me. Eventually, they went back to the games they were playing.

"You wouldn't have to save me, though. My man would," I assured her.

"Speaking of this man, you love him?" she asked me.

It was evident that we loved one another, but I wanted to hear it out of his mouth, and I wasn't saying it first. Even once those words were exchanged, I still couldn't meet his daughter because Peaches would be in the way. When I did get pregnant, was he going to love Rhea more than our daughter, if we had one? I had a million what ifs and not enough answers. Ship was starting to feel scary to me because I was at the point where I wouldn't be okay if I lost him. I was in the thick of being in love. It was the turning point of loving him more than I loved myself.

"A lot." I nodded my head. "And that shit is scary as fuck," I told her, not wanting to go into details.

"Are you scared that he's not the one, or are you scared that the shit is too perfect?" She raised her eyebrows at me.

"Both," I confessed.

Suddenly, people started saying their goodbyes and leaving. I was confused.

"Party ending already?" Michelle asked.

"Yeah, we ain't feeling it," Denver said.

"The fuck does that mean?" I asked.

"It means, y'all ain't come in here and speak to nobody but daddy and Michelle. Vince feels some type of way and so do I," Denver said as she let the last person out the door. "Y'all can go," Denver said, looking at me and Michelle just as Daddy and Ship were walking in from the back.

"What's the problem?" Daddy asked.

"I'm sorry," Michelle said. "Is Vince living here?" She scrunched her face up.

"Come on, Ship. We outta here," I told him, knowing that my daddy was fitna go off.

"Been living here, gon' keep living here, and ain't nobody gon' do shit about it," Vince went off.

"Little nigga, who the fuck you think you talking to?" Daddy rushed over to Vince, but Denver blocked him.

"I'm talking to all y'all. I pay all the bills in this bitch. Denver don't work no fucking where. So, yeah. I live here. She ain't no little ass girl. She's a grown ass woman," Vince said.

"Vince, please stop. That's my dad," Denver pleaded with him, but it was too late. He was already on a roll. "Daddy, he just drunk. I'm sorry." Denver had her hand on Vince's chest, trying to keep him back.

"I ain't tryna hear none of that shit!" Daddy yelled and Michelle got in front of him.

Denver and Michelle were both standing in between my father and Vince.

"Why the fuck you just standing there?" Denver yelled at me.

"That's where she need to be. She and that bitch ass nigga she came with can leave."

Ship swung on Vince, and he stumbled. I dropped my shit at the door as Denver hit Ship.

"Bitch!" I grabbed her by her hair, pulling her backwards on the floor. "Keep your fucking hands to yourself!" I held her down, not wanting to hit her.

It wouldn't be our first fight. We'd gotten into plenty. Some she won, but most I won. She couldn't fuck with me. I glanced over, and Ship was kicking Vince in his face.

"That's for my bitch windshield!" Ship yelled.

"Ard, I think he's had enough," Daddy said to Ship.

My father pulled Ship off of Vince. Vince spit blood onto their carpet. His face was swollen, and he couldn't get to his feet.

"Y'all get out of here," Daddy said to me and Ship.

I shoved Denver one last time and headed for the door.

"Daddy, you always let her get away with shit. They came in here, rude as fuck," Denver whined.

"This motherfucker ain't supposed to be living here. I told you I ain't want no nigga up in here every day. This your fault!" I heard him yell as Denver's screen door shut behind us.

"You good, baby?" I asked Ship as we rushed down the steps.

"Hell yeah," he answered, getting into the car.

Ship sped off and adrenaline pumped through me. I was feeling my liquor and my nigga. Watching him beat Vince's ass turned me on. I wanted him to handle me in the worst way. I hadn't given him any all weekend. At this point, I was torturing myself.

"Aye, why was you in there drinking like that when you might be pregnant?" he asked me.

The thumping in my pussy died. Way to kill the fucking mood. Ship and I agreed that I wouldn't take another pregnancy test until the end of next week. I couldn't fight the urge, so I took one earlier this morning. Another negative. That's part of where my attitude with him came from. His focus should have been on putting a baby in me. Instead, Rhea was his number one priority, as she should be, if she was actually his daughter.

"I took a test this morning," I confessed. "It was negative," I mumbled.

"Ok, well. I'll bust in you tonight." Ship shrugged.

"Ship, it don't work like that. I have to be ovulating," I told him.

"You been following that period tracking shit for weeks, and it ain't worked. Fuck that shit. We just gon' fuck until we get a positive. That drinking shit is dead, though."

"You already took smoking from me. Now you trying to take drinking, too? Like, what am I supposed to do to manage my stress?"

"What you got stress from?" he asked.

I debated on if he was ready to hear the truth or not. I was stressed about us. That's probably why I wasn't getting pregnant. My period was all over the place. And part of me felt like he was throwing my shit off because he was fucking two bitches. I knew that wasn't true, but it made me feel better to put it all on him.

"You're giving Peaches too much control in our relationship. I feel like I'm going to lose you because you're mistaking my dislike for Peaches for me not wanting you to be around Rhea. And that's not the case. I want to meet her. I'm ready for you to meet Demari, too. But not if I don't know for sure that you're going to be here."

"I said I want this." Ship glanced over at me as he drove. "Like you've asked me a million ways. And you keep asking me. If you ain't going to believe me, then stop asking me. I want you. I want the five kids. All of it. Like, what I gotta do for you to believe I love you?" he asked.

There it was. Ship finally told me out loud that he loved me. I didn't want to cry, but I couldn't help it. It's like I knew it already, but hearing it out of his mouth made it real.

"Girl, what the fuck is wrong with you?" He let out a deep breath.

"You said you love me," I cried.

"You act like you ain't never heard me say that shit before. You sure you ain't pregnant? My sister, Schetta, was crying just like that when she was pregnant." He brought his eyebrows together, confused.

"No, I'm not pregnant." I bust out laughing. "But no, you haven't said it," I told him, wiping my eyes.

"Oh. Well, I love you, I love you, and I love you some more," he said.

"I love you, too."

"You better because you working a nigga nerves too much to be playing with my feelings and shit," he said.

"Demari acts just like me, so we fitna be working your nerves together." I bust out laughing.

"I get to meet your son?" Ship asked.

I nodded my head, smiling. "I'm nervous as fuck about it, but I think it's time. You gonna be here. I want you here. You've seen a lot of me, but you haven't seen me as a mother yet. I think that's important. You've already met his dad. *And* with us planning to have a baby, it's best we start pulling our blended family together."

That was my way of telling him that it was also time for me to meet Rhea. I'd give him the freedom to make it happen on his own. But it had to happen. I thought it was important that me and Peaches sit down before I met Rhea. He knew that, too. He needed to be thinking about all of that.

Me and Ship hadn't spent any real time together, just the two of us. I didn't want to overwhelm him. It almost felt like I would be pressuring him to get to know me. Having a relationship with my brother was important to me. That didn't mean that it had to be important for him. I finally blocked my worries out and reached out to him. I mentioned grabbing some food, and he was with it. Me and grandma were in the living room, watching her court shows, waiting on him to get here.

"Taniyah, what the fuck is wrong with you?" Grandma snapped on me.

"What?" I asked.

"You shaking my whole damn coffee table. Why you got ya foot on it anyway? Take all that jittering shit up in your room, shit."

"Me and Ship hanging out today. I'm kind of nervous," I admitted.

"You ain't going on a date with the nigga. He's your brother. Just act like he one of them girl-bros that you be talking about." Grandma laughed at her own joke. "Them boy-girls," she added on, laughing even louder.

Slang had always been lost on Grandma. When I said *bruh* she thought I was literally talking about a guy. I didn't think I was a guy and neither did my friends. It was just how we talked. Part of me thought she knew that, and she was just trying to be smart. I was going to be smart, too, and keep reminding her.

"My friends don't think they're guys. We're just lesbian studs. That's it."

"In my day, we called the lesbians that wanted to be boys, dykes. If you want someone to know you're a woman, then you'd dressed like a woman. You dress like a boy because you want to be seen as masculine. Am I wrong?" She raised her eyebrows. "You doing the bending, right?" Grandma continued asking questions, though I hadn't responded to anything. "Oh, 'cause it felt like you thought you was teaching me something. I don't care how many pussies you eat; I know what the fuck I know." Grandma rolled her eyes at me.

A knock at the door, saved me from the embarrassment I felt. Grandma believed that the perception you gave off showed your intentions. If you knew you'd be called a hoe for wearing a skirt with no panties, you'd put some panties on at the bare minimum. Otherwise, you wanted to be seen as a hoe. Because at the end of the day, that's what the world would see.

She argued that she didn't care what I wore out of the house, but she was going to call it what it was. Definitions didn't change because I was her granddaughter. In her eyes, I wanted to be perceived as a boy. If I didn't, I would find some comfortable women's clothing. There was no explaining it to her because at her big old age, she was who she was.

I opened the door. "What's up?" I dapped Ship up, trying to walk straight out the door.

"Hold up, yo." Ship laughed. "I wanna see Grandma," Ship said, moving forward, forcing me to back up.

"She got an attitude," Grandma said.

"Hey, Grandma." Ship leaned down to give her a kiss on the cheek. "What you got going on?"

"Watching my shows. I'm sure glad you taking your sister on out of here. I can get some peace and quiet," she hollered out.

Ship laughed but wasn't shit funny. At this point, she was agitating me on purpose. I hated when she did that.

"You started talking to me," I defended myself. "I was minding my business."

"What you was doing was shaking my damn coffee table!" Grandma looked back at me. "Girl wants your approval so bad, she acting stupid."

That was taking shit too far. I walked out of the front door, embarrassed that she called me out. It wasn't that I wanted his approval. I was confident in who I was. I did want him to like me, though. At thirty-two, I knew how childish it sounded. But I wanted to be myself without having to explain it all the time. I wanted me and Ship to be as close as the other siblings that grew up in the same household. I was still a girl. I never pretended to be a boy.

"You driving. A nigga tired." Ship said, walking out the door.

"Ard," I mumbled.

"Aye, shake that shit off. I want you to like me, too," he said, tapping me on the shoulder.

That was a pick me up. I was nervous and Ship was, too. He seemed so calm, cool, and collected. Even when he met Pat, he was chill, like he'd seen the nigga a million times before. It would all be simple if I could just get out of my head and just be regular.

"How long have you and Nevada been together?" I asked, making conversation.

"Not that long, for real . It feel like forever, though. I fuck with her. Real bad. Like, I wanna marry her and put a bunch of babies in her ass." Ship laughed. "Shit tricky with my baby mother, though. I'm tryna figure out how I can blend the shit together, so we can be one cohesive unit."

"Nevada not with it, or your baby mother not with it?" I asked him.

"They just got some lil' shit going back and forth. They ain't had no words or nothing like that. If I felt like I could get them in a room just to talk, I'd do that, but I don't know, for real . Like, it's a long story. But I'm meeting Nevada's son soon. I already met his father. It was a little slight exchange, nothing heavy. I met her whole family at this point. She's trying to move in that direction. I just don't want her to quit on me because I'm not moving fast enough for her. And I don't want Peaches to feel like I'm trying to boot her out the picture either."

"What you feel about a little get together? We can do a little dinner at Grandma's. She can meet your daughter and Peaches. I'll bring my girl. Everybody can get comfortable. It'll let Peaches know that she's still your family. So, when you pull her and Nevada together, she won't be in her feelings."

"I can fuck with that." Ship nodded his head. "Since you got all the answers, how the fuck do I tell Nevada that I'm taking my baby mother to meet my grandma on some family shit?" Ship twisted his lips up.

"I don't have the answers for that one, bro."

We both fell out laughing. Ship and I grabbed lunch from a sport's bar, chatting it up. He talked about his upbringing, and I shared mine. To hear the way he felt about his mother, put me in my feelings. Feelings that I'd only let go a few months before meeting Ship. God did that for me. Maybe he could do that for Ship, too. If Ship was willing to give God a try.

"How you get over all that childhood shit?" he asked.

"I'on know." I shrugged. "I woke up one day and didn't want to feel that shit no more. I met this older woman at my car shop. She introduced me to God. I visited her church once. Didn't go back for a few weeks. And now I go every Sunday. I guess He just took it from me." I shrugged. "The last thing I asked him for was that he start revealing my siblings." I raised my eyebrows.

"And poof," Ship tossed his arms in the air, "here I am."

"Nah." I laughed. "It's wild how it happened. The nigga that usually cuts my hair got killed. So, that's how I ended up in the shop Nevada worked in. I was tryna get at her. So, I gave her my business card. When she called, I thought it was my chance to shoot my shot. Whole time, she bringing me my brother." I laughed. "I don't wanna say the nigga got killed so I could find Nevada 'cause God could've just moved him out of state or something. Had him retire early. I don't know." I shrugged. "But it's definitely a good example of one door closing and another one opening."

"Hell yeah. I done talked your ear off about my girl and my baby mother. What's up with your girl?" he asked.

"We been kicking it going on three years. She works at a daycare. She been on me about moving in with her. But I ain't feeling that shit." I shook my head.

"Yeah, I feel you on that. Moving in together is where you see a bitch true colors." Ship nodded.

"It ain't even that for real . I trust her. But I ain't meet grandma until I was eighteen. She ain't young. I wanna get as much of her as I can, even though she gets on my nerves sometimes."

"I feel that. But she a phone call away. A visit away. Moving in with your girl ain't knocking grandma out your life. But refusing to move forward with your girl might have her leaving you."

"She be threatening that shit all the time. I can almost hear her putting me out whenever she gets mad. I ain't tryna deal with that shit either. With Grandma, she can talk all the shit she want, but she ain't ever putting me out on the street."

“Putting a nigga out be the first go to with bitches. But when you free for this dinner shit? The sooner the better,” he said. “Before my bitch leave me.” He laughed.

“Shit, we can do it tonight.”

“That’s a bet.” He nodded.

We left the bar with full stomachs. At the house, he jumped out of my car and into his. We agreed to do dinner at seven. So, it would only be a few hours before he was back.

I called my girl from the car before going in the house.

“Hello?” Amiya answered.

“What you doing tonight?”

I hoped my brother ain’t get mad when he found out that grandma hates my girl. I kind of sold it to him that it would be a smooth night. That was some shit that I couldn’t promise. The food would hit, though, because I wasn’t cooking shit. I was ordering in. Good food usually made people happy.

Ship

"Hello?" Peaches answered my FaceTime.

"What you and Rhea doing tonight?" I asked her.

She was at the kitchen sink, washing Rhea's hair.

"Hi, daddy!" Rhea yelled, waving, even though she couldn't see my face.

"Hey, daddy's baby. You getting your hair washed?" I asked the obvious. "I know it's going to be pretty."

"Mmhmm," she said back.

"I'm about to put some braids in her head. But that's all we got going on. You wanted to come see her?" Peaches asked.

"Nah, I wanted y'all to meet my grandmother and my sister," I told her.

"For real ?" Peaches faced the screen with a smile.

"Mommy!" Rhea yelled.

"Oop, I'm sorry, baby." Peaches turned her attention back on my daughter like it should have been in the first place.

"Daddy, mommy got water in my ear!"

"I saw it, baby."

"But yeah, that's cool. Send me the address, and we'll be there." Peaches said.

"Bet. And don't be wearing nothing crazy. My grandma real

vocal, and she gon' check you," I warned her.

"Ship, get the f-word off my phone!" Peaches hollered back.

"What f-word, mommy?"

"Freedom. Like Harriet Tubman led the slaves to freedom," Peaches answered her.

"Nice save!" I called out to her before ending the call.

Nevada was at work. It'd been a while since I'd shown my face in the shop. So, I popped up on her ass. I couldn't risk Peaches posting another picture on social media. Nevada needed to know what was going on straight from my mouth. I was hoping since she was at work, she wouldn't show her ass too much about it.

"Hi, baby." Her smile lit the entire room up as the bell chimed at me walking in.

I walked through, dapping up all the niggas I knew, which was damn near everybody. When I made it over to Nevada, I kissed her cheek.

"Take a break," I told her.

"She can take a break after she finishes my shit," the big nigga sitting in her chair, spat.

I tried to be respectful to motherfuckers. But there was always some slick talking nigga who thought he was bigger and badder than me. A nigga chilled the fuck out, but I was still reckless as a motherfucker when I needed to be. It felt like niggas were testing my gangsta too much lately. Nevada dug in her customers ass before I had a chance to.

"Bitch, don't talk to my nigga like that. I ain't doing shit now. You can get your fat, funky ass out my chair!" Nevada pulled the cape from off of him.

I laughed in that nigga's face while finishing off my

Snapple. I took the empty bottle to the side of his head.

"Get your bitch ass up!" I barked in his face. "Fuck wrong with you, nigga?"

"Ship." Nevada pushed me out of the front door. "Relax."

"Who the fuck that nigga thought he was talking to?!" I pushed the shop doors open.

"It don't matter. You already hit the nigga. What's up? You stopped by for a reason. Or you just wanted to see your baby?" she asked, wrapping her arms around my neck and kissing on me.

"I was coming to tell you something." I wrapped my arms around her waist so when she tried to pull away from me, she wouldn't be able to.

That fat bitch came walking out the store, scared as a whore. He rushed in the opposite direction from where me and Nevada were standing.

"Ok, so what's up?" she asked.

"I'm taking Rhea to meet my grandmother tonight," I said. Nevada's face went from confusion to anger.

"That ain't what you tryna tell me." She tried to pull away, but I had her tucked in my arms. "Just say the shit, Ship. I gotta get back to work."

"Peaches is going to be there, too."

"See, there's the bullshit. Get the fuck off of me." She tried to pry herself out of my grasp.

"Why you tripping? I'm not picking them up or none of that. She's meeting me over there. I want my grandmother to know Rhea. I want Rhea to know her. Introducing them gives Peaches some support with Rhea when I'm not around. You should be happy about it in a way," I suggested.

"And I can't go?" she asked.

"I ain't say that, but—"

"Then, I'm coming," Nevada told me rather than asking.

I debated on telling her ass no. Telling her she could come would lead to more bullshit with Peaches. A nigga was always having to choose between their asses. The shit was giving me a headache.

"Ard." I sighed. "I'll pick you up at 6:30," I told her.

"I know you will."

When she tussled for me to let her go, I didn't fight her this time. I watched her switch that fat ass into the shop. A nigga should've just lied and stuffed Peaches's phone in the trunk. That way, she couldn't get any pictures. Peaches wasn't going to be with none of this shit.

∞∞∞

As expected, Peaches wasn't trying to hear it. A nigga waited till the last minute to warn her that Nevada was coming. She whipped her car around before I could explain myself.

"This your shady ass way of trying to introduce *my* daughter to that Desert Bitch! I already told you that I'm not wit' none of that shit. You not fucking slick. I'm not meeting you no fucking where, and Rhea is staying right here with her mother. You keep fucking playing with me and you won't see Rhea at all," Peaches went off. "You keep throwing that bitch in my face. I get it! You got a girlfriend now. Well Rhea has another father now, too!"

The next thing I heard were three beeps, signaling that the call had ended. Both these bitches were driving me crazy. A message from Peaches popped up on my phone.

Lyin Ass Bitch: And send me gas money for wasting my motherfucking time!

I finally found a girl who didn't belong to another nigga. Like, she was mine. But I had to prove myself at every fucking turn. She didn't trust me for shit. And Peaches wanted to pretend that it was still me and her. But she hadn't tried to fuck me at all, so I don't know what the fuck she wanted really. I never thought having more family would bring me more problems. A nigga never had family issues before.

"I'm ready." Nevada got in the car.

I was on the phone, sending Peaches her gas money before she tried to keep Rhea from me. It was starting to feel like a nigga rushed into this shit with Nevada. I should've given Peaches more time to warm up to the idea of me having a bitch. I needed to move the right way now that Rhea's real dad was in the picture. Just thinking about that nigga around my daughter made my chest tight.

"You rushed me because you said we were going to be late. Now you taking time out to send ya baby mother some money. Ain't you 'bout to see her?" Nevada asked.

I knew she could see my phone because it was sitting in the car mount. I didn't bother to try and hide it from her. It was her fault I had to send the money anyway.

"No. I'm not about to see her." I glanced at Nevada before hitting send on the fifty I sent to Peaches.

It wouldn't take but thirty to fill her tank, but maybe she would lighten up with a few extra dollars in her pocket.

"What happened?" Nevada asked.

You happened. You and them dumb ass games you playing with my baby mother. That's what I wanted to say, but I bit my tongue.

"I told her you were coming, and she wasn't wit' it. That's also why I had to send her gas money," I mumbled.

I buckled my seatbelt and pulled out of the space.

"And you're blaming me?"

"It ain't nobody else's fault," I said.

"You can take me the fuck home." Nevada's thumb pointed behind us.

"You got me fucked up. You invited yourself along. Fucked everything up, and now you talking 'bout I can take you home? Hell nah."

"I fucked everything up?" Nevada asked.

"Yeah, man! This dinner was to make Peaches feel included while introducing Rhea to my grandmother and sister. It wasn't to show that you with me. She knows that already. After this dinner, I was going to put something together for the two of you to meet. So, we could come to a common ground or something. But y'all so fucking childish, it ain't gon' happen."

"That's your fault for carrying on secret fucking plans. I'm not a chess piece that you can move around however the fuck you see fit. You don't need to plan my life. I want to be included when you're making the plan. Or at least filled in. If you had said that when you told me y'all were doing dinner, I would have fell back," Nevada said calmly.

"Why a nigga gotta say anything? I tried to do the right thing by letting you know. Why that's not enough? I ain't did shit for you not to trust me. I want this shit to work as bad as you do. Probably more. But it feel like you just want me to cut Peaches out of my life, and I can't do that. I won't do that," I told her.

"You ain't did shit? The pictures this bitch kept posting of you. Every time you didn't show up for me, it's because you were with her. She was making it look like y'all were together. So, if you mad that I don't trust you, take that shit up with your baby mother. I'm not no crazy bitch just pulling shit out of thin air."

"You got it in your head that a nigga want that bitch. Or that other bullshit you keep saying about me playing into her hand and shit. That's a game that you two motherfuckers playing. That shit ain't got nothing to do with me. She's Rhea's fucking mother! What you want a nigga to do?!"

"Figure it the fuck out! You the man. That's *your* baby mama. I'm *your* girl. It's on you to figure it out. But this ain't working for me. And it ain't working for her either. So, you sad? Too bad, us too," Nevada spat, folding one arm into the other.

I ran my hand down my face after parking in front of Grandma's. The last thing I wanted to do was a fucking dinner. Especially when I wasn't showing up with the star of the show, my daughter. I wasn't in the mood. Nevada was in a worse mood. I should have let her ass go home when she suggested it.

"Come on," I said to her, getting out of the car.

Nevada grabbed my hand as we walked up Grandma's steps. I gave her hand a quick squeeze. She made her way under my arm as the door opened.

"Bro, what's up?" TJ opened the door wide for us. "How you doing, Nevada?"

"Hey, I'm good." Nevada stepped in front of me.

"Where's your daughter?" TJ asked.

"Her mom had something to do," I lied.

I learned enough not to let everyone know the bullshit you had going on in your relationship. You would get over it, they wouldn't. TJ led us into the kitchen, and Nevada and I immediately looked at one another. I'm glad my daughter wasn't here for this bullshit.

Nevada

"What the fuck wrong with the two of y'all?" Ms. Ada asked.

Me and Ship looked at Amiyah. When we were on that *Smoke with Me* show, it was down to me and her. I would never forget her face because I thought she was going to win.

"How long have y'all been dating?" I asked TJ.

"Three years," TJ answered, looking back and forth between me, Ship, and Amiyah.

"Mmm," I mumbled, taking a seat.

Ship took the seat next to me, shaking his head. If either of us was going to tell TJ about Amiyah, it should have been Ship. It was his sister after all. I wasn't even invited. It wasn't my place. If Amiyah had any decency, she would fess up before we had to tell on her.

"Well, spit it out, nigga," Ms. Ada said to Ship.

"Ard." He ran his hands back and forth in his head. "You know the show *Smoke with Me*?" Ship asked TJ.

"Nah, catch me up."

"You don't have social media?" I asked her.

"Nah. I don't mess with that stuff. That's how you get in mess," she answered.

Mess had seemed to find its way to her anyhow. It was crazy

because Amiyah was sitting there, eating, like we weren't fitna blow her spot up. The bitch didn't have a care in the world. I guess she didn't care about TJ as much as TJ cared about her. I mean, she was at the girl's grandma's house for an introduction dinner.

"Ard, well. That's how me and Nevada met. It's a little local dating show where you decide if you wanna smoke with a motherfucker or not. Nevada was in the final two and I chose her," Ship explained.

"He chose me over Amiyah," I finished the story.

"You finally gon' leave that trash alone or what?" Ms. Ada looked to TJ.

Her elbows were on the table.

"Here we go." Amiyah let her food fall onto her plate.

"What you mean, here we go?" TJ asked. "You going on dating shows and shit?"

"I wasn't on there looking for love. My sole purpose was to be seen. Increase my following so I can start making some money off of social media. That's it, that's all." Amiyah made the period motion with her hand.

"You said you could picture him on your dick," I added.

"For reaction," Amiyah defended herself. "When that shit hits the internet, motherfuckers are going to come looking for me. I'll be getting followers left and right." Amiyah shrugged.

"At what cost, though? Embarrassing me on the internet?" TJ scrunched her face up.

"Y'all can do that shit outside. It's time for that bitch to go," Ms. Ada chimed in.

"You wanna argue about something?" Amiyah stood from the table. "Let's argue about how disrespectful your grandmother is. She been calling me bitches and hoes since I met her. And you let her. Ain't nobody cheating on you, but I don't think anyone would blame me if I did." She grabbed her purse and headed for the door.

TJ stood around. She bit her lip. "I'll be back," TJ mumbled before turning to leave the kitchen.

"Going to give that bitch a ride home, ain't you?" Ms. Ada asked. "Soft ass."

"How else she going to get home?" TJ called out before slamming the front door.

"Bitch could've taken a Lyft. Your sister is a little girl dressing like a man. All she do is let these little bitches play with her the same way men do. I don't know why she just don't go and get a dog. And least the motherfucker would love her back," Ms. Ada said, getting up and leaving the kitchen.

"You ready?" I asked Ship.

"I don't think I have a choice," Ship responded, standing.

The car ride home was quiet. I think the both of us were still feeling the argument we had on the way to Ms. Ada's. I wanted to get to the other side of this baby mama drama. He did, too. But neither of us knew how to do that. I mean, I knew how, I just didn't want to give in. I couldn't be with a man who had no control over his baby mother. Especially when it wasn't even his baby. I wasn't letting that go. Ship could easily fix all this between us by not dealing with Peaches anymore, but he wasn't going to let Rhea go. I understood it, but I wasn't willing to look past it. Peaches was a problem. He knew it, too.

"I think I'm going to stay at my shit tonight," Ship said.

"I think that's a great idea," I agreed.

"Whatever, man." Ship shook his head. "Talk to you tomorrow."

"Maybe."

He shook his head in frustration. Ship ran his hand down his face before unlocking the door. I didn't want to give him an ultimatum. That was the fastest way to lose a nigga. But I was a woman worth keeping, too. His thoughts should have been focused on not losing me as well.

"I only got one more time in me, Ship. The next time you choose Peaches over me, that's it," I told him as I opened my door.

"I'm choosing Rhea!" Ship yelled. "You keep making it about that bitch, and it ain't about her! I'm always going to choose Rhea. Over you. Over Peaches. Over my fucking self. So, if you going over that, then go. That ain't some shit I'm willing to change."

"There's a difference. What you're doing is pacifying Peaches so you can have Rhea. Where does it end? Huh? One year into our relationship? Three? Ten?! Give me a number and baby, I will thug that shit out. I promise." I held my pinky up for him to attach his.

He didn't. He looked away, staring out the fucking window like the answer was out there somewhere.

"Exactly. You can't do that because you don't know. I don't have the answer either. What I do know is that you are willing to do that shit forever. If this is what being with you is going to be like, I don't want forever. I don't even want right now. I need some space until you figure out what you want," I said, getting out of the car.

"I know what I want. But, I hear you. I don't know what I'ma do, but I'ma figure it out," Ship said.

"I hope you do because I love you."

"I love you, too." Ship rested his head against the headrest.

I shut the door, fighting tears as I walked away from him. I made it to my building doors before a tear finally fell. I could see Ship in the reflection of the glass, staring at me. He looked like what I felt like.

∞∞∞

It'd been a few days, and I hadn't heard from Ship at all. It wasn't like I reached out and he ignored me. Until this shit with his baby mother was fixed, we wouldn't get anywhere. Our arguments were getting worse. I didn't want to do more damage. So, I was staying out the way.

I kept Demari home this weekend, despite him begging to go to one of his grandparent's house. Now that school was out, his ass was never home. He went from one grandma to the next one. Sometimes, they did exchanges without anyone telling me. I wouldn't know until I called him. I knew all of my grandparents, and I wanted Jemari to get the same experience. I spent full summers only talking to my mama and daddy on the phone. But I missed my son.

Admittedly, I knew it was coming from being in my feelings about Ship. So, what.

I was laying across the couch when a knock at the door scared the fuck out of me.

"I get it, ma. That's probably my dad." Jemari walked past me with a basketball in his hand.

"Where you going?" I asked him as he opened the door.

"You ready?" Jemari stepped inside of my apartment. "What's up, baby mama."

"Hey. Ready for what? Ain't nobody told me nothing." I looked at the two of them.

"Boy, I told you to ask your mother." Jemari smacked Demari in his head. "We going to do a little bit of everything," Jemari told me. "Father-son day."

While I was happy Jemari was spending more time with our son, I had planned to do a mother-son day. He was stepping on my toes. He could be father of the year another day.

"Well, that's why somebody should have said something to me because I planned a mother-son day. I missed my baby. I was thinking Five Guys for lunch, then maybe we could go laser tagging, get you some new shoes, and then dinner and a movie," I offered Demari, hoping he'd rather spend the day with me.

"Sorry, dad. I think I'm going to go out with mommy."

Oh, to be a kid again, where you could just be honest and let the adults deal with their emotions behind it. I was the adult with all the emotions now. The shit wasn't fun. But I was glad I beat Jemari out.

"Well, daddy was going to take you to Smashburger, a little basketball. Then, we were going to go to the mall and get you fly like me." Jemari popped his collar like this was the early two thousands. "Then, we were going to do some paintballing before going out to eat."

"Dang," Demari said.

He rubbed his ear, confused. I think we were both feeling bad now, because before I could tell him to go with his dad, Jemari suggested something else.

"Aye. We family, right?" Jemari looked from me to Demari. "Why don't we all go out? And we do whatever you wanna do, Mari. If that's cool with mommy's boyfriend."

"Boy, shut up." I sucked my teeth. "Whatever Mari wants to do."

"The three of us," Mari said excitedly.

"Ard, I'm driving, though. Your mama think the curb is a part of the road," Jemari said, letting Mari out of the door first.

"She don't be hitting the curb no more." Mari laughed. "She do be backing into the small poles at the gas station, though."

"I did that one time," I defended, locking my apartment up.

Walking down the steps with them, I couldn't help but feel that this was the exact shit that I was mad at Ship about. I would be mindful not to take any pictures that would suggest there was more going on between me and Jemari. This was about Mari hanging out with both of his parents.

I played princess passenger while Jemari drove from place to place. Mari chose Smashburger for lunch. We slid bowling in after that. Jemari won both games and I was at the bottom. Paint balling was right after that. I didn't suit up because I didn't trust Jemari with that damn gun. He wouldn't miss an opportunity to get a good shot to my ass. If I were playing, I would have landed one right between the eyes of the shield that covered his face. I got some good pictures of them.

This was my first time experiencing Jemari and Mari like this. He made some time for his son. I was glad he did. They were having such a good time that I knew this would be the turning point of Jemari showing up the way he was supposed to. Even if he just grabbed him for a few hours, it'd be an improvement. My baby had been smiling so hard that it was making me smile. I loved this for him.

I let them do their thing while shopping for clothes and shoes. It was always my responsibility alone. But watching Mari interact with his father, I realized this should have always been there thing. It was a completely different experience than when I was helping him pick out clothes.

While we drove from dinner to the movies, I couldn't help but think about how great the day had been. We hadn't gone out as a family since Mari was almost two. I wanted this. But I wanted it with Ship and our son that would look more like him than me. Or our daughter that would for sure be a daddy's girl, the same way Rhea was. I wanted in on his life.

By the time the movie finished, we were all worn out. Jemari's old ass fell asleep midway, and Mari and I clowned him the entire ride home. He damn near kicked me out the car when he pulled up at my apartment. Mari was going to stay the night with his dad.

"Let me talk to you for a second," I told Jemari as I got out of his car.

"I be right back, Mari."

Jemari met me on the sidewalk a little ways from the car. We were close enough to see him while being far enough away that he couldn't hear us.

"Today was dope, for real . I don't think I've ever seen you be a father the way you did today. Our baby is so happy." We glanced at him in the car.

"Yeah. I ain't gon' hold you. I loved it. I wanna do it more. It wasn't that bad hanging out with you either," Jemari joked.

"I'm still the cool ass bitch you met," I reminded him with a laugh. "I think you should take over the shopping for clothes and shoes and shit. You were better at it than me. I'll still pitch in on the price tag.

"And you were great with letting him get a little dirty when we were paint balling. I think you should join us next time."

I scrunched my lips up, feeling like the conversation was starting to go in a different direction. I meant what I said. Today was great. But it hadn't turned me on any towards letting Jemari hit again.

"Girl, I ain't mean it like that. I told you I don't want your ass. Just giving you your props." He held his arms up defenseless. "Maybe next time, ya nigga can come, too. My girl. Everybody could be one happy family."

I didn't even know if Ship and I were going to be together. Hell, we could've already been broken up. That wasn't Jemari's business, nor was it my business that he had a girl now. So, I would ignore the way he slid her into the conversation like I already knew about her. It didn't matter. As long as we loved on our son, we were allowed to move on.

"Maybe. Y'all have a good night. And my baby don't need shit else to eat," I said, walking up my building steps.

"Shit, girl, we fitna go to Waffle House right now." Jemari bust out laughing, getting back into the car.

When I made it into the building, I heard his car pull off. In seconds, I was back in my apartment, alone and wanting to cry. I jumped in the shower, as if the falling water would hide my tears. I missed my man. Real bad. But if I budged on this, I'd be adjusting to Peaches's wants forever. I had to have faith that it would all work itself out. God hadn't brought us together just to break our hearts later.

Stepping out the shower, I didn't feel any better. But my tears stopped. I lotioned down and cuddled against the empty space that belonged to Ship. His scent was starting to fade from my pillowcases. My phone chimed just as I drifted off. Ship texted me.

Big Ship: Meet me at Texas Roadhouse tomorrow at 8. I love you.

I smothered my face in the pillow as I screamed with happiness. It felt like I would never talk to him again. There was no telling if he actually figured shit out, but he thought he had. That meant he was trying. I didn't doubt that he was. But confirmation was everything.

Peaches

Ship telling me that he was bringing Desert Bitch to dinner really pissed me off. Like, what would possess him to slide her ass in at the last minute? He was giving her too much control. And that was a problem because all she wanted to do was get me out the picture. He couldn't see it because he loved her. Yet, the nigga could see all my flaws. It was making me feel like he didn't love me anymore. The only reason I was going to meet his grandmother was because of Rhea. All she had was me and Ship. I wanted her to have as much family as possible.

He did apologize for the way he went about it. But he made it clear that Desert Bitch wasn't going anywhere as well. So, fuck that apology. I wanted that bitch out of here. The more he tried to push her into our lives, I would push Rhea's imaginary stepfather into the picture.

"Daddy!" Rhea ran to Ship as he walked into my house.

"Don't be walking in here without knocking. This my s-word," I told him.

"What s-word, mommy?" Rhea asked, hugging tightly to her father.

"Salty, baby," Ship answered before I could. "The chicken is salty."

I tossed Ship the middle finger when Rhea wasn't looking. He stuck his tongue out at me. That shit made me drop my attitude and bust out laughing. I didn't hate his ass. I wanted to, but it was hard. He hadn't done anything to me that I didn't deserve. Though, I didn't know he wasn't Rhea's dad. I didn't tell him that she could be someone else's either. That was my bad. I just wished his feelings hadn't changed so much and so quickly.

"Daddy, where we going?" Rhea asked as we walked out of the front door.

"It's a surprise." He tickled her a little before sliding her into her booster seat.

"Daddy, you know I can't do this." She played with the seatbelt strap.

"Girl, snap yourself in that seat and stop playing with me." I whipped my neck around at her.

Rhea poked her lip out and snapped herself in. She gave me a little eyeroll, and Ship popped her thigh immediately.

"Don't be rolling your eyes at your mother," he said, shutting the door.

By the time he made it into the driver's seat, she had burst into tears. The pop didn't hurt. Getting corrected by her father had crushed her like an eighteen-wheeler.

"Cut all that crying out. Ain't nothing wrong with you," I told her, unaffected by her tears.

Ship, on the other hand, was about to go into convulsions. He couldn't take making her cry. When she got her first shots, he cursed the doctor out. He started with, "I'm sorry, ma'am," and ended with, "y'all got me and my baby fucked up," storming out of the room.

I watched his jaw unclench and his grip on the steering wheel loosen as Rhea stopped crying. I told him if he didn't get that under control, he'd be helping her hide bodies. He argued that he was going to do that anyway. His number one goal as a father was to always be there for her. He never wanted her to get into a situation that she felt she couldn't call him. He didn't care how ugly it was.

I wasn't nervous until Ship parked. It'd always been just him and his brothers. I never had to worry about someone in his family liking or not liking me. Desert Bitch was one thing. At the end of the day, he could get a million more girlfriends. He couldn't get another grandma. He wouldn't since he was twenty-nine and just finding her.

"Daddy, this ain't no toy store." Rhea lifted herself from her booster seat a little, looking around the neighborhood.

"Who said we were going to the toy store?" Ship looked back at her.

"You said it was a surprise," she whined.

"It is," he assured her, getting out of the car.

As expected, he took her out of her booster and kissed her all over her face. That was the make up for snapping on her when we first got in the car. The man was hard up in the streets but soft as tissue when it came to Rhea. That's why Desert Bitch couldn't have him.

Ship led the way up the steps with Rhea in his arm. She pretended to braid his beard. I snapped a picture just for keepsake because I wasn't allowed to post them on social media anymore, which I thought was bullshit, but I had to choose my battles wisely. The imaginary daddy thing would only take me so far. I could only use it when I knew for a fact that it would count.

The front door opened to a stud girl with a big ass smile on her face. Rhea immediately laid her head down on Ship's chest. I watched her grip tighten around his neck. Our family had been our family since she was born. It was rare that we were in an intimate space like someone else's home, and she didn't know the people in the room.

"What's up, bro?!" His sister excitedly dapped Ship up. Their dap ended with Ship pulling her close to his chest.

"Rhea, this is daddy's sister, TJ. TJ, this is my daughter, Rhea," Ship introduced them.

"Hey, niece. Nice to meet you." TJ held her hand out for Rhea to shake.

She reluctantly stuck her hand out. She looked at TJ weirdly. I knew what my baby was thinking. She couldn't figure out if TJ was a girl or a boy. It was obvious to us but to a little kid, she had no clue. She heard Ship say sister, and she heard TJ's voice. But her clothes and her name didn't match up to what she knew about boys and girls.

"This is Rhea's mom, Peaches. Peaches, this is my big sister."

"How you doing?" TJ extended her hand out to me.

Now that she was right in my face, I got a better look at her. She and Ship could be twins, they looked so much alike. She was literally the girl version of him but really the boy version because she dressed like one. She was thicker than him but still, they looked like they came from the same nut sack and coochie.

"I'm good. Nice to meet you." I shook her hand, smiling.

"Patrick, you better not be walking in my door without my grandbaby this time," I heard an older woman call out to him.

"I got her." Ship laughed.

We stepped into the living room to see his grandmother. I was stuck. I quickly pursed my lips, knowing my mouth was hanging open. He looked just like this woman. Like, if I had never laid eyes on his mother, I would think his father made him on his own. This shit was wild.

"Grandma, this is Peaches, my daughter's mother. Peaches, this is my grandmother, Ada," Ship introduced me first.

"What's your real name, girl?" She frowned at me.

"That is my real name," I told her.

It was rare that anyone asked me for my real name. I'd had all the same doctors, dentists, etc. for years. They already knew. Anyone around my age that I met, didn't question *Peaches* because they assumed it was a nickname. I hated to see that the embarrassment of having to explain that hadn't changed at all.

"Oh, lawd," Ms. Ada said, rolling her eyes at me.

"It's amazing how much Ship looks just like you," I said, changing the subject.

"That's how DNA works," she said plainly, scrunching her face up at me. "Why doesn't this little one look anything like my grandson?" she said aloud.

We hadn't been standing in the living room for longer than five minutes. She noticed it immediately. I guess I should've been grateful that he didn't have a grandma all those years ago. She seems like a woman who would've made him get a DNA test the same day that I pushed Rhea out.

"It's a long story that I don't want to tell in front of *my* daughter," Ship interrupted.

"Well, ard. If it's out there already. I'll shut up." She waved her hand in the air.

"This is Rhea, my daughter. Rhea, that's daddy's grandma. So, she's your great grandma." Ship said, trying to put Rhea on her feet.

She kicked her legs, making small sounds that she didn't approve.

"How old is this girl?" Ms. Ada asked.

"Five," Ship answered.

"And too damn old to be doing all that nonsense. Put her ass on her feet. You can walk, right?" she said to Rhea as Ship put her down.

She clung to Ship's leg. She held a finger in her mouth, staring at Ms. Ada.

"Oh, girl." Ms. Ada waved her off. "I guess you don't want none of them crabs in the kitchen." Ms. Ada pursed her lips up.

Ship must have told her all of Rhea's favorite things. I think crabs was at the top of her list. Honestly, I felt it was more because the adults were excited about them, than she actually enjoyed the taste. She just wanted to be doing big girl stuff, except for when it came time to pick through them.

"Can I have some crabs?" Rhea switched her usually loud voice for a softer tone. One I could barely hear.

"Well, first you got to take that finger out your mouth," Ms. Ada told her. "Then, you got to come and give me a hug."

Rhea creeped over to Ms. Ada, hugging her. Ms. Ada stood, scooping Rhea into her arms. She whispered something in her ear as they walked to the kitchen. I don't know what she said, but Rhea nodded her head, smiling.

"Aye, I'm sorry about that. My grandma don't bite her words," Ship offered me an apology.

"Yeah, she can be a lot. It won't be the last time either," TJ joked with me.

"It's fine. Now that I know, I'm prepared." I smiled. "Can you show me where the bathroom is? I wanna wash my hands."

"Yeah, come on," TJ said.

Ms. Ada's house was one of the older houses on this block. Hers was built before half baths were a thing, I assumed.

"Bathroom is right there. You can find your way back into

the kitchen, right?" she asked me.

"I'm sure I can. Thank you," I said, stepping into the bathroom.

She might not have had a half bath, but the one she had was huge. I'd love a house with a jacuzzi tub. I gave my hands a quick wash and rushed back downstairs. At the kitchen doorway, Rhea sat next to Ms. Ada.

"She gonna pick her own crabs. She gotta learn some time. Now look…" Ms. Ada explained to Rhea how to open the crabs.

This was nice. Ship and TJ wore smiles, watching Rhea learn. She wasn't scared of cutting herself either. Ms. Ada was going to be a fucking handful, but she'd love my daughter. So, I'd take the tongue lashings. I glanced at Ship, and he was staring at me. He nodded his head for me to walk further into the living room as he walked over to me. Ship looked like he had something to get off his chest.

"My grandma is good with Rhea," Ship said as we watched them from the living room.

"She is. Rhea could use some independence," I agreed.

"Good. Tomorrow night at eight. Me, you, and Nevada are going to Texas Roadhouse to talk," he said. "Grandma can watch her."

"What is it about this bitch that you keep shoving her down my throat?" I whisper yelled. "Like, I get it. You've moved on. I don't need to know her." I sucked my teeth, folding my arms across my chest.

"But you need to respect her." Ship raised his eyebrows at me. Before I could get to cursing his ass out, he started talking again. "And she needs to respect you."

"Or, I can keep pretending that she doesn't exist," I suggested.

"You can't do that." Ship ran his hands down his face.

"And why not? You have to fuck her not me," I argued.

"Because I love her, Peach," Ship whispered.

I knew he loved her. It showed on him. She had such a big effect on his body that I could see when he was going through it with her. I'm not sure why him confirming what I already knew broke my fucking heart.

Ship

I sat in the restaurant, waiting for Nevada and Peaches to arrive. Hoping they would arrive, rather. Both of them tried to tell me when they would be ready for me to pick them up. I burst both of their balloons when I told them I wasn't picking them up. They were both children. So, I had to treat them as such. Neither of them was getting a ride because then they'd be throwing it in the other one's face.

A nigga ain't know if this shit was a good idea. All I knew was that I missed Nevada. And that I wasn't reaching out to her until I had a plan. She said I had one more time to fuck up and she was done with me. I didn't want to lose her. So, regardless of how this dinner went, I was coming to her with my best.

Peaches wasn't left out either. This was for her to get a chance to speak her peace, too. This shit could work but only if the two of them let me be the man in the situation. They both wanted control and tonight, they had to pass that shit to me. I was surprised when Peaches walked in first. If I had to put my money on which of them wasn't going to show, I wouldn't put it on Peaches. She was gaining the least from this shit. She didn't have to hear me talk to know that.

"Everything was cool when you dropped her off to my grandmother?" I asked her as she took a seat.

"I mean, she took her." I shrugged. "I don't really know what it's like dropping your kid off somewhere so." She shrugged, laughing.

"Grandma ain't give you no smoke, did she?"

"Of course she did." I rolled my eyes. "I don't even care. I'm just happy to be kid free tonight. I don't even know what to do with myself." She smiled.

I didn't see Nevada walk in, but Peaches's face told me. That smile was immediately replaced with the dirtiest look I'd ever seen. This was their first time seeing one another in person. I imagined the first look would be a little uncomfortable for everyone. As long as they didn't get to throwing hands in this bitch, we were good.

"Hey," Nevada said, sitting down.

I was relieved that she hadn't come in here, trying to slob me down. I missed her ass, but now was not the time. All I wanted to do was get through this uncomfortable dinner. I wouldn't label it a success until we sat through an appetizer and dinner. Even though them being in the same room right now, calmly, was a win in itself.

"Peaches, this is Nevada, my girlfriend. Nevada, this is Peaches, my daughter's mother," I started with the obvious. "In a perfect world, this is how the two of you would have been introduced. A nigga fucked up." I tossed my hand in the air.

"You did," Peaches mumbled.

The waitress walked over just in time. She asked for our orders. Surprisingly, Nevada and Peaches both ordered something. This was already going better than I thought it would.

"I shouldn't have called you in the middle of the night and told you about Nevada the way that I did," I explained to Peaches.

"You shouldn't have," Nevada chimed in.

"Ard, I'm trying to take accountability. I don't need y'all gaining up on me." I looked at the both of them. "The point is, I'm trying to fix it. I don't know what that shit looks like. But if we leave this table and everyone is happy except me, I'm okay with that."

When the waitress came out with the two appetizers, Peaches dug in first. She used a fork to take food from the center and put on the saucer. Nevada dug in behind her. I was feeling hopeful.

"So, I think first, y'all gotta squash y'all petty shit, and then we can talk about y'all expectations of me," I said, stuffing fries into my mouth.

"I didn't start shit," Nevada said.

"If we get into who started what, we not going to get nowhere. Fuck it, just state what your issue is, man." I ran my hands down my face.

Trying to get either of them to accept accountability wasn't going to happen. I had to move this shit along before one of them got up to leave.

"It's clear she don't want me around," Nevada started.

"Can you address her?" I asked Nevada.

Nevada let out a deep breath, rolling her eyes at me.

"It's clear you don't want me around. It started with you tagging him in pictures with Rhea."

"You hear her?" Peaches looked at me. "She has a problem with me tagging you in pictures of your daughter. I knew that shit came from her when you told me.

"That's not what she's saying, and you know it," I defended Nevada, twisting my lips up at Peaches. "You were making it look like we were together. Motherfuckers in the comments amping us up like we in a relationship and you loving the commenting but not telling them what it is."

"Because she is trying to erase us from your life!" Peaches was getting upset.

"No, I'm not! But Ship is my nigga," Nevada jumped in. "There has to be boundaries. You threaten him with Rhea's real dad to get your way. It's fucked up because he loves you. Rhea, too. And me. And I love him, so I can't sit by and watch you play with him. It's not even all about what your bullshit is doing to our relationship. It's about you manipulating him to get your way."

"And you don't manipulate him?" Peaches said, swiping her tears away like it was a fruit fly that landed on her. "Somehow you managed to slide your way into a dinner where me and Rhea were supposed to be meeting his grandmother," Peaches argued.

Nevada looked away.

"Yeah, so let's not act like you not doing shit, too!"

The waitress came to the table, placing our plates in front of us. Even if she hadn't heard the yelling coming from our table, she had to feel the tension. It was thick. Together, we passed her the trash from the appetizer and waited for her to leave our space.

"Ard, man. I don't want to lose either of you. Nevada, I want to be with you. And Peaches, I want to be there for you when it comes to Rhea, like I always have. So, how do we move forward? Peaches, what do you need from me?" I asked her.

"You told her that Rhea isn't yours?" Peaches asked, too upset to look at me. She angrily twirled her pasta onto her fork.

"No," Nevada answered for me. "He told me that Rhea has another father. But he has consistently told me that Rhea is his. He's made it clear that she will always come before me. And for the record, I don't have a problem with that."

"Well, since everyone knows, I need it to stop coming up. You're telling that story like I tricked you or something. I didn't know either," Peaches said.

"I can do that." I nodded my head.

"I'll never mention it again," Nevada agreed.

"Your grandmother, too. You can tell her the truth, so that she stops mentioning it but after that, I don't want to hear any more about it," Peaches warned.

"I'll talk to her tomorrow," I assured her.

"And outside of that, I just want to know that Rhea has you. If you have more kids, if you and Desert Bitch, I mean, Nevada go get married in the morning, I want to know that nothing changes between you and Rhea. Regardless of what either of you think. Anything I've done is to make sure Rhea keeps Ship as a father. She loves him more than she loves me."

"Can't nobody come between me and Rhea, not even you," I told her.

She laughed a little, nodding her head. "I can adjust then."

"Thank you." I let out a sigh of relief. "Nevada, what you need from me?"

"I need to know that the family we're trying to create is a priority, too. But more than that, I need Rhea to be a part of what we're building." Nevada looked to Peaches. "I love Ship. And in loving him, I have to love everything he loves. Even if I don't like it. And I haven't met your daughter, but I love Rhea, if nothing more than because she's his." Nevada looked at me. "I want her to be there for family moments. I want us all to be able to come together for her birthday and Ship's. I want her to have a big brother in my son and be a big sister to whatever me and Ship create together. I can't have all of him if Rhea isn't allowed around me. I promise I won't hurt your baby." Nevada's eyes watered. "Ever." She wiped her tears.

"I can do that." Peaches nodded her head, wiping her own tears.

"Thank y'all." I ran my hands down my face, trying not to cry myself.

These bitches legit loved a nigga. If they were being real, then this shit could work. We shouldn't have no more issues. Just as we settled into our new co-parenting shit, the unbelievable happened.

"Your waitress had a family emergency, so I'll be—" The waitress paused, making me look up from my phone. "Patty?" She scrunched her face, not sure she was seeing what she thought she was.

It was my mother. I hadn't seen her ass in some years. And when I did, it was never more than a quick glimpse before I walked in the opposite direction. I'd take a longer route home to avoid her ass. If she hadn't said my nickname, I wouldn't have known it was her.

She was thicker than she'd ever been. Well, in my moments with her. Her face was clear, her lips were moistened. She looked...healthy. I didn't have to ask to know that she was clean. Looked like she'd been sober for a while. I thought hell would freeze over before that ever happened. So, I didn't really know what to say to her.

"What's up?" I asked her, clearing my throat.

"How you doing?" she asked.

"I'm straight," I answered. The thought crossed my mind to ignore asking her the same thing. But if she wasn't using, then she wasn't the bitch I couldn't stand. "How you?" I asked.

"I'm doing great," she said. "Been clean for a year now. Just got out of the halfway house and into my own place. I've been asking around about you," she said.

"Oh, yeah? I'm not hard to find," I told her, lifting my arms up, looking around the restaurant. "What you want with me?" I couldn't resist asking.

When I was younger, I'd be at Kiss or Kong's house for days. The bitch never came looking for me. I always knew where to find her ass. Somebody's trap house. Or in an abandoned building, getting high.

"I wanted to tell you I'm sorry. Maybe be your mother again, if you need one, still."

"I don't," I told her.

"Ship," Peaches and Nevada said at the same time.

"I'll let you all finish your meals up." She pursed her lips, embarrassed. "See you before you leave?" Nadine asked, hopeful.

I ain't say shit and let her walk off. The shit was weird. We never had a mother-son relationship. Seeing her was like seeing my old crossing guard. There was nothing there. And I wasn't about to fake that shit for her or nobody else.

Peaches and Nevada looked like they had everything to say. Neither of them said shit, though. They just looked at their plates.

"So, neither one of y'all gon' ask me what I need from y'all? That's fucked up." I shook my head like I was truly disappointed.

"You need to go talk to your mother," Peaches mumbled.

"Mmhmm," Nevada moaned in agreement.

Ship

"Wrong answer," I responded. "What I need is for y'all to trust me." I looked back and forth between the both of them.

Nevada and Peaches nodded their heads. Nadine came back over with to-go boxes. On the inside of mine was a piece of paper with her number written on it. Nevada hurried to snatch the paper up. She saved the number in her phone.

"Just in case you try to throw it away." Nevada smiled.

"Smart." Peaches nodded her head.

Getting these bitches to come to a common ground had done nothing but allow them to gang up on me. I'd rather them both be against me than to be against each other. I was a smooth ass nigga and could talk my way out of anything. I tossed some cash on the table, and Peaches double checked the bill.

"Oh, you want to contribute something?" I asked her as we stood.

"I'm just making sure you left her a good tip," she said.

"I got a tip. Mind your business." I scrunched my face up at her.

Outside of the restaurant, we agreed on a date where Nevada could meet Rhea. Peaches would be there with us. Once that was out of the way, Peaches would be okay with Rhea staying out with me. Peaches got into her car and pulled off. I walked Nevada to her shit.

"Did I fix it?" I asked her, leaning against her door.

I pulled her into me and wrapped my hands around her waist. Nevada kissed me a few times before resting her head onto my chest.

"You did. Thank you," she said.

"Thank you for being patient with a nigga."

"I think we should go to my house and be real patient with one another." She looked up at me, placing more kisses to my lips.

"Hell yeah." I squeezed her ass. "Beat you there."

"You gon' have to let me go." Nevada laughed as she was still in my grasp.

"Never," I told her, staring into her eyes.

"That works for me," she said. "Now move." She pushed me, jumping into her car. "See you!" she yelled out as she pulled off.

She was really trying to race a nigga to the crib. What she didn't know was that no matter where we were, I would always get there faster because I took the backroads everywhere. I made my way to her apartment. A nigga thought he was working all of that over time because Nevada and I were planning to have a kid. Turns out, it was to buy Nevada a ring. I was going to marry this bitch.

She managed to make it to her apartment before me. As I stepped into her building, I found her stuff all throughout my walk to her apartment. Both of her orange Dunks, then her socks. A T-shirt, then her leggings. Her thong hung from the knob of her front door. Her bra was the last thing I found before I found her.

She was legs wide open on the kitchen counter. She played with her pussy, twirling her fingers around her clit. I was rock hard, coming out of my shit. Ass naked, walking over to her.

"Time for dessert," she moaned, intensely staring at me.

I took a seat on the bar stool. My hands pulled her by her thighs to the edge of the counter. I played with her, licking her clit slowly while staring up at her.

"Stop playing and eat that shit," she begged.

She tried to hump my face, but I moved it away just as she got too close.

"Ship!" she yelled, tossing her head back. "Please," she cried. "I ain't felt that tongue in days. I need it." She looked down at me.

"You need it?" I asked her.

She nodded her head, face frowned like she was upset.

"I need it," she whispered. "I need it," she moaned.

I moved my face towards her, ready to slowly devour her, and she grabbed me by my neck. Nevada's other hand held my head in place as she wound her hips against my mouth. Her juices coated my lips like marinade.

"I'm cumming!" Her legs shook. "Suck it out of me, please, baby!"

Nevada had a trembling orgasm on my tongue. Her humps got slower. Her grip on my head and neck loosened as she tried to come down from her nut. Before her body could relax fully, I was sliding my dick up in her.

Thrusting in and out of her, quickly, Nevada kissed me. Her panting into my mouth had me ready to nut already. It'd been days since I had her good stuff. She had a nigga weak in the knees. Nevada pushed me out of her, jerking my dick. She climbed down from the counter. On the walk to the coffee table, she twirled my dick in her hand, almost making me cum.

"Bust in this pussy, baby," she said as she spread both cheeks as far apart as she could. Yeah, I could fuck her ass for the rest of my life.

∞∞∞

Later in the week, I was meeting up with Nevada to meet Mari for the first time. I even set an alarm so I wouldn't be late. The plan was to be early. Kong was over the crib, kicking it with me and Kiss.

"So, them bitches ain't get to scrapping?" Kong asked.

"Hell nah. They were both crying." I laughed. "Oh, and our waitress had a family emergency. Guess who the new waitress was? Nadine," I answered before they could guess.

"Nigga, you lying." Kiss whipped his neck around from the game.

"I wish I was. She looked good, though. Said she been clean for a year. Bitch put her number in my to-go box. Nevada hurried to put that shit in her phone 'cause she knew I was going to toss it." I laughed.

"Call your mother, nigga," Kiss said to me.

"Man, you ain't gotta call her ass. How many times she called you?" Kong asked. "Never," he answered his own question.

"You only get one, yo," Kiss said. "Call her while you can, nigga."

"I hear you," I told him.

I felt where Kiss was coming from. His mom had cancer and if she didn't recover from it, she would die. But Nadine wasn't a good mom like his was. I could've gone my entire life never seeing her again and been cool. Now that she had reappeared, I did wonder if it was for a reason. Since getting with Nevada, I don't know. It seemed like I was getting blessed with more of everything. Like she was my good luck charm or something. A nigga ain't know how to move with Nadine yet, but I knew that Nevada had the number if I ever did want to get to know her.

"What happened with that surrogacy shit? Is Schetta gon' do that shit for her aunts?" I asked Kong.

"She was going to do that shit behind my back. But when she took her ass down to that doctor's office, her ass was already pregnant. Haaaaaa." Kong stuck his tongue out his month.

"Congratulations, my nigga." I dapped him up.

"Thank you, thank you. The big man can go ahead and give me my little girl now, and then I'm going to get snipped. I don't want no more of these motherfuckers," Kong said.

"I should've gone and got snipped." Kiss shook his head. "Cambria pregnant, too."

"Nigga, you lying," I said in disbelief.

"I wish I was. A nigga got caught up in that news about my mother. Bust all up in Cambria. Stupid fucking nigga," Kiss said to himself.

"We about to have kids at the same damn time?" Kong asked.

"Not if I can talk her the fuck out of it. We can't afford no more kids, and I don't want no more attachments to her ass," Kiss said.

"Don't ask her about no abortion, nigga. You never gonna get the same bitch back. She ain't ever going to forgive you," I warned him.

"I don't give a fuck. I don't want to do this shit. Fuck I look like having a kid while my mother dying? I ain't feeling it."

I didn't want to press the issue. For once, I knew better than Kiss. He could act like he hated Cambria all he wanted. But at the end of the day, he wanted his family. He would for sure lose them if he asked her to get an abortion. The nigga had enough going on, so I let him be.

"I'm thinking about asking Nevada to marry me," I confessed.

"Nigga, you known that bitch two months," Kong argued.

"It's been like six. And when you know, you know." I shrugged.

"Bitch, if you get married, then Schetta gonna want to get married," Kong said.

"And what's wrong with that?" Kiss asked.

"I'm not tryna sign no contracts and shit. You get married to get divorced. I like shit just how it is. Her ass ain't going nowhere. She ain't too demanding. Bitch suck a nigga dick every day. The second we say *I do* all of that shit changes. Hell nah. Marry her in secret or some shit," Kong said.

"Y'all nigga talk to Tessa?" Kiss asked.

"Hell nah."

"I'm not thinking about that bitch no more. I love Reagan, but I got my own shit going on. Ain't like Mont left on the best terms anyhow. I can't be chasing behind that bitch to let us love on her daughter." Kong waved it off.

"I don't give a fuck about the bitch either. But I love Reagan more than I hate her mother. I don't know what Mont was going through to crash out how he did. But that's still my brother. If one of you niggas dipped on me, I would make sure your kid was good," Kiss argued.

"I'll never see y'all kids hurt, but what the fuck we supposed to do if the bitch don't want us around?" I threw my arms up.

"I don't know but something," Kiss mumbled.

"Nigga full of shit. You don't want your own kid but wanna take care of Mont's." Kong had the three of us hollering. "Niggas is crazy."

My alarm went off, signaling that it was time for me to go. I dapped them niggas up and headed out the door. Nevada wanted me to meet them at the bowling alley we went to on our first date. It took me all of twenty minutes to pull up in the parking lot. I was early like I wanted to be. Peaches called me just as I saw Nevada pull up. Her timing was the fucking worst.

"Hello?" I answered.

"Ship," Peaches cried into the phone.

"What's wrong with Rhea. Is she alright?" I asked.

"I don't know where she is. Help me find my baby!" she yelled in my ear.

That confession made my mind go blank. I swear, my soul left my body. A nigga was just there. No feeling, no thinking, no seeing. I was just a shell.

"Ship!" Nevada slapped my arm. "What the fuck is wrong with you? I'm trying to introduce you to—"

"Rhea is missing," I cut her off. "I gotta go."

I jumped in my car and pulled off, leaving Nevada and her son standing there. She'd just have to understand. I ain't want Mari or her to see me like this. I was about to murk Peaches.

Nevada

"Come on," I told Mari, running back to my car.

"We not going laser tagging?" he asked, whining.

"No," I said.

Ship drove through the city like a lunatic. I was keeping up with him as he bent corners with his foot pressed heavy on the break. Red lights appeared as I zoomed through the yellows. If the speed camera caught me, fuck it. I'd worry about that later. It was always something. But Ship and I agreed that we were in this together. So, if his daughter was missing, mine was, too. It was one hell of a way to be introduced, but we had to work with the cards that had been dealt to us.

I was right behind Ship as he pulled into an apartment complex. He parked, and I was parked right beside him. Peaches was standing there, talking to the police. Ship walked over to my car.

"What you doing here?" he whispered at my window.

"You said Rhea was missing. I came to help find her," I told him.

"That was sweet. It's why I love you. That's why I'm going to marry you. But you do not want to see the nigga I'm about to turn into. And even if you can handle it, I don't want your son to see me like that. Not the first time meeting him at that. I know what you were doing, and I appreciate it, but go home," he pleaded with me.

Ship didn't look angry. My man looked hurt. Scared even but not angry. I wasn't leaving him. Mari saw worst shit with his father. He'd be fine.

"Mari, this is mommy's boyfriend, Patrick." Ship sighed. "Patrick, this is my son, Demari," I introduced them.

"What's up, man?" Ship looked through me to the back seat.

"Nothing. Your daughter missing?" Mari asked.

"Yeah." Ship nodded his head.

"I hope we can find her," Mari said.

"Me too." Ship nodded his head at my window.

He stayed there, not talking until the police started leaving. I rolled the windows up, leaving Mari in the car. Ship looked harmless before, but now he looked like he might kill Peaches.

"You tell them police about Rhea's father?" Ship asked her.

"What?" She scrunched her face up. "No," she answered.

"Well, where the nigga live at? I need an address or something," Ship pushed.

"He doesn't have her, Ship. Please do something more productive than asking me stupid fucking questions."

"How the fuck you know he ain't got her? You don't know that nigga!" Ship roared.

"Because he's in fucking California!" Peaches screamed with tears streaming down her face. "He was here that one time. He went back home, said he wanted nothing to do with Rhea. I've been lying this whole time. You can yell at me about it later. Right now, we need to find my baby." Peaches jumped into her car.

Ship looked as lost as he did when we were in the parking

lot of the bowling alley. He thought he had a lead on where Rhea might be. Hearing that her father wasn't actually around, had him lost all over again.

"We're going to find her." I held his face in my hands.

"You don't know that," he said, knocking my hand away from him.

"Daddy!" a small voice yelled from the curb, and the two of us whipped our necks in that direction.

Rhea was yelling his name from the back of a police car. Peaches parked her car, running to Rhea. Ship squatted down in place, running his hand down his face. I can't imagine the relief he felt in that moment. Peaches was on her knees in the dirt, holding on to Rhea. Rhea was trying to pry herself away from her and get to Ship.

Peaches finally let her go, and Rhea came running over to him. He scooped her up and spun her in a circle, holding her head to his chest. Peaches slowly made her way over. You could see the guilt on her face from the games she had played. We were silent in the moment, just happy that Rhea wasn't kidnapped or worse. The officer was walking over to us.

"She was down the street, playing with someone's puppy. We would've missed her if the woman hadn't flagged us down. Everything is alright. You folks have a good night," he said, walking off.

"You too," I told him.

"Thank you!" Peaches called out to him.

"Why would you walk off like that?" Ship asked her.

"I saw the puppy. I was yelling for the lady to slow down, but she didn't. I wanted to pet that dog," she said, smiling.

"That was dangerous. You know better than that," Ship

said, unamused.

Rhea burst into tears, and Ship didn't budge. "I don't want to hear it. Kill all that noise," he told her.

She slowly stopped crying. "Hi." I waved at her. Her tiny hand waved back at me.

"That's daddy's girlfriend. Her name is Nevada. And that's her son over there in the car." Ship pointed.

"You're so pretty," I told her.

"Thank you," she said, still upset with Ship for going off on her.

"You wanna stay with Daddy tonight?" he asked her.

"Yes." She played with her fingers.

"You don't just get to decide that. You still need to ask me. She's *my* daughter," Peaches stood in front of Ship.

"Take me to court and prove it," he told her. "Meet you at the laser tag spot," he said to me, kissing me on the lips before walking off to the car.

Ship had the upper hand with Peaches's confession. We all sat around that dinner table, agreeing to put our differences aside. I wasn't sure how much I trusted that she would do that. Now, we'd never have to find out if she was going to keep her word or not. She had no choice but to cooperate. Ship was all she had.

Still, I felt bad for her. When we were going to bed tonight, after I fucked the shit out of him, of course, I was going to talk to him about it. He didn't need to be an asshole to her. Human decency wasn't a reward for good behavior. The least he could do was ask if he could take Rhea for the night.

"I bet you're real fucking happy," Peaches mumbled to me.

"And here I was, thinking that I would talk Ship into not going too hard on you for being a fucking liar. You can forget that shit now," I said, walking off to my car.

"We going to laser tag now?" Mari asked.

"Yep. You wanna do me and you versus Patrick and his daughter, girls versus guys, or parents versus kids?" I asked him.

"Girls versus boys!" he yelled excitedly.

"Oh, that's how you feel?" I asked him. "Bet." I nodded my head, laughing with him.

When we made it to the parking lot, Ship was tossing Rhea up in the air and then catching her. After parking, I snapped a picture of them. I see why Peaches snapped so many pictures of them. It was literally the cutest shit ever.

We walked through the parking lot with our kids holding hands and the two of us on the ends of them. I glanced over at Ship to see him already looking at me.

"What?" I mouthed.

"I love you," he mouthed back.

I mouthed back the same, throat burning because I was choked up. I didn't know what I wanted from a man, just that I wanted someone to lay my ass up against. Somehow, I ended up with so much more than I ever could have asked for. I loved this nigga, and I couldn't wait to pop some babies out for him.

We played a few games of laser tag. The last round was Ship and I versus the kids. Rhea wasn't any help, no matter who she was paired with. So, we let them when the game so they could celebrate their win together. Leaving laser tag, we walked over to Outback for some food. The two of them ordered chicken tenders like most kids did. Rhea told me all about her coloring books and puzzles. Mari told Ship about his basketball skills and the music he liked to listen to. I don't know how Ship knew any of the new rappers that Mari was naming because I was still listening to music from the nineties and early two thousands.

When we made it home, the kids were worn out. We let Rhea have my bed while Ship and I were cramped on my sectional. My little two-bedroom apartment wasn't big enough for the family we already had. It damn sure wasn't going to be enough to bring three more kids in here.

"So, you think we should get a place together?" I asked him.

"This two-bedroom shit ain't going to work. I don't think we have a choice." Ship kissed my cheek.

"What about Kiss?" I asked him.

"Oh, now you concerned about my friend?" he joked. "Nah, but Kiss will be straight. That nigga always good. He'll understand, and he'll figure it out."

My phone vibrating on the coffee table got our attention. It was only 10 p.m., but we had a long day. And on top of that, it was emotional. It felt like two in the morning.

"It's Denver." I rolled my eyes at the phone and put it back on the table.

"Answer the phone," Ship said, climbing over me. He started getting dressed.

"Where are you going?"

"To your sister's," Ship said, pulling his shirt over his head. Ship typed quickly on his phone before grabbing his keys.

"Huh?" I was confused. "She's not calling anymore."

No sooner than the words left my mouth, Denver was calling again. I sat up, answering the phone on speaker.

"Hello?"

"Help me!" Denver cried into the phone.

"I'm on my way!" Ship called out before rushing out of the apartment.

The phone beeped three times, and my throat went into my stomach. I wanted to run behind him, but the kids were here. Ship was involving himself in my sister's bullshit. Women in domestic violence relationships didn't always want to be saved. She could flip on him, and Ship would be getting jumped on by Vince and her. I had to be there.

I slid my leggings back on. When I burst into Demari's room, he was wide awake, playing the game.

"Get dressed, we gotta go."

Demari could see the fear on my face. Without argument, he dropped the remote on the floor. In my bedroom, Rhea was knocked out, snoring and all. I scooped her into my arms, managing not to wake her up. Mari opened the front door for me and locked it behind me.

I got Rhea into her booster seat. "Snap her in, Mari."

I shut the door, jumping into my driver's seat. Speeding off, I headed to Peaches's place. I impatiently stopped at red lights and stops signs, zooming through yellows until I was outside of her apartment. I frantically knocked at the door.

"Who the fuck is it? And why the fuck you knocking on my door like that?" She talked shit from behind the door.

"It's Nevada," I said.

"What's wrong?" Peaches snatched the door open.

Her face looked how I felt. "Is Rhea okay? Where's Ship?" Peaches walked out of the house barefoot. She went over to my car, calming a little when she saw that Rhea was okay.

"Rhea's fine. Ship is helping me with a family emergency. I need to be there. I didn't want to take Rhea, so I brought her to you."

"Ok." Peaches nodded.

A mix of worry and confusion showed on her face. When she opened the door, her eyes landed on my son.

"Hi," she said, offering a small smile. "I'm Rhea's mom. You ok?" she asked.

"You mind keeping him for a few?" I blurted out.

I don't know where that came from. I didn't know what else to do. There was no time to make more stops. Denver needed me. Ship might need me. And Demari would be safe right here with Peaches at least until Jemari got here.

"Sure." She nodded.

"Thank you," I said. "Demari, I need you to stay here with Rhea's mom, okay? I'm going to call your father to come pick you up. I trust her. You're safe, okay?" I assured him as I held the back door open for him to get out.

"Okay," he said.

"Peaches," I started, but she cut me off.

"I got him, go," she assured me.

I nodded, getting into the driver's seat and pulling off. Peaches was a liar. She played a lot of fucking games. But she loved her daughter. And she loved Ship. She wouldn't hurt my son, if for nothing more than the fact that Ship would be done with her ass. Peaches was a mom, so she had to know that I'd blow this whole fucking complex up if she played with me.

Dialing Jemari, I sped through the backroads to get to Denver's. He answered on the first ring.

"Mari good?" Jemari asked, half sleep.

"He's fine. I'm going to send you an address. I need you to

go pick him up. Denver is into it with her boyfriend, and I need to go over there. Mari is with Ship's baby mother. I just dropped him off," I explained.

"Ard. Shoot me the address," he said.

"Thank you."

I ended the call with him. Stuck behind a passing train, I took the opportunity to send Peaches's address to Jemari. The second the gate lifted, I sped over the tracks. Tears poured, blurring my vision with the thought that I wouldn't get to my sister in time.

Peaches

In the midst of trying to get Rhea and Mari in the house, Rhea woke up.

"What you doing in my house, Mari?" She asked him.

"Rhea, stop being rude!" I snapped on her.

"My mom said I have to stay here until my dad gets here." He explained to her.

Mari took his shoes off at the door; pulled his switch from his backpack and was already comfortable on the couch.

"Tell Mari, good night." I told Rhea.

"I wanna stay up with, Mari," she whined. "That's not fair!"

He wasn't going to be here much longer. I figured there was no harm in letting Rhea stay up. I turned the TV on. She climbed onto the couch, sitting next to him, laughing at the cartoon.

Giving Rhea another sibling had never crossed my mind; I was good on having any more kids. One was more than I could handle because quite honestly, I was selfish as fuck. However, watching her with Mari, I wish I'd given her that. When Ship and I were done and gone, she would only have herself. Starting over at this point would be insane. So, I was glad she found a big brother in Mari. I could count on him being around; because it didn't seem like Ship and Nevada would be calling it quits any time soon.

"I'm going to be right out front, ok?" I said to them, opening the blinds before I left out the front door.

I needed to smoke. It had been one hell of a day. It's like we were one big happy family in a matter of a few hours. Nevada leaving her kid with me wasn't a light matter. Like, we were really doing this. No sooner than I took my seat, a car parked right in front of my door with their headlights beaming. When the lights turned off, Jemari got out of the car.

"Aye, I came to get my son." He said, not realizing it was me until he got right up on me. "Peaches?" He scrunched his face up at me.

"What's up?" I laughed.

"I ain't seen ya ass in forever." He leaned down to give me a hug. "That shit crazy," he ran his hands down his face. "You Ship's BM." He nodded his head.

"In the flesh," I replied, knowing it was a lie.

The truth wasn't his business, though. It did make me feel good that Nevada had called me Ship's baby mother when she knew the truth. She'd stated at the dinner, that we would never again discuss the fact that he wasn't, and she was keeping her word.

"You know what we say out here; the city is big but,"

"Baltimore is small," we recited simultaneously.

I watched Jemari's face change. When he first walked over, he was giving me a genuinely confused but happy look. Now he was looking at me with wonder. Wondering what I'd look like when I arched it. Wondering what I felt like – taste like. He was interested and I hadn't offered anything.

I had already looked him up and down; ending up big disappointed that he didn't have sweats on. It had been years since we graduated, and I couldn't remember if he had a big dick or not. What I did remember is that he always had a bitch.

That memory inserted itself just as I was wondering why I never fucked with him back them.

He was standing in front of me now and I wanted to take him for a ride. It was a line I wouldn't cross, though. Nevada and I were just getting on the same page. Something like fucking her baby father would come off as petty when really it was just curiosity.

"How you feel about your baby father dating my baby mother?" He asked.

It didn't really surprise me. I knew the conversation was headed there. As long as I didn't end up with his dick in my mouth at the end of the night, flirting was cool.

"I'm over it now." I laughed, passing him the blunt.

"Now? So, I take it you was on my baby mother's head?" he laughed.

"She just became Nevada tonight. Before that she was Desert Bitch!" I confessed.

"You ain't even the first chick to call her that shit." Jemari shook his head with a smile on his face.

Damn! He even had perfect teeth. In high school the nigga always wore a gold grill, two or three chains, and he always had a stack of cash in a rubber band. I looked at his pockets to see that hadn't changed.

"How you feel about her dating Ship?" I asked. "Jealous?"

"Please!" He passed me my blunt back. "I don't want that girl. And to keep it real, I fuck with Ship – on the strength that Mari fucks with him. I trust my kid more than anybody else. If he say the nigga good, then he good." Jemari shrugged.

"That's mature of you. Not the Jemari I remember from high school at all." I acknowledged who he used to be.

"Niggas grow up eventually. I'm even thinking about being a one-woman's man, now." He smirked.

"Is that so?" I rolled my tongue around the inside of my bottom lip. "What made you decide that?"

"Mari. I spend way more time with him now. The little nigga watches everything I do. I want my son to have a wife and a family. Ion want him fuckin' on everything and get stuck with the baby mother from hell. Ion want the nigga to get so caught up in these bitches that when he is ready to settle down, it ain't shit but hoes and gold diggers left."

"Is that what you're stuck with?" I asked him.

"Ion know. You a gold digger?" he asked me with the sexiest set of *'come fuck me'* eyes that I'd ever seen on a man before.

I couldn't even lie to myself like that shit didn't warm my body. Still, I wasn't going to cross that line with him.

"Ion think we should go there. This shit complicated." I looked at our kids through my front window. Rhea had fallen asleep with her head on Mari's lap. Mari had fallen asleep with his head on the arm of the couch and his gaming switch in his hand.

"The way I see it, it's easy. Our kids know each other already – we know the other parent already. The only way it could fuck up is if we fuck it up," Jemari said, inching closer to me with each sentence.

He had a point; but what he left out was if Nevada would have an issue with it. Pissing her off was equivalent to pissing Ship off; and he was already mad at me for lying about Fresh being around for weeks. I was already on his bad side, but I deserved loved, too. I was getting ahead of myself because Jemari hadn't said that he was interested in more than sex. While I craved a good orgasm, my rose could get it done quicker and save me the headache. Moving forward, I needed clear communication of a nigga's expectations. That's not to say I wasn't down to fuck still. A bitch just wanted to know if it was just sex.

"Are we talking about sex? Or are we discussing kicking it and fucking around – seeing where shit goes?" I asked.

"A nigga do wanna fuck! I ain't on no hit it and quit it shit, though. But we ain't linked up since high school, for real; we gotta get to know each other all over again. You might not be feeling a nigga. I'm falling back from the streets so my money different," he explained.

"I'm not a gold digger," I retorted.

"Even a bitch with her own bread want a nigga to take care of shit. I'm just saying, I might get to know you better and not be feeling you. We might not vibe so a nigga ain't fitna tell you he ready to run off into the sunset. I can assure you that you ain't got to worry about taking no L's with me – we got too much on the line," he looked at our kids through the window.

"That's exactly why we shouldn't even play with fire." I countered.

"But it sure is pretty to look at." He whispered.

Jemari had a point. Fire was magnificent to look at; until it was burning your house down. I wasn't trying to jump into no relationship or a fuckship, but I wanted someone, too. Ship had lucked up and found Nevada and I was honestly happy for him. But that didn't mean it felt good being on the outside looking in. I wanted someone to love me.

Ship

I knew this call was coming. I'd been waiting on it, honestly. When Denver jumped on me to defend that bitch ass nigga, I knew then that he was hitting on her. At the very least, she was scared of him. If she had stood there and let him get her ass beat, he would've taken it out on her. He probably still did. I wasn't a fan of Denver's. I didn't like the bitch at all to be real, but my bitch loved her, so I had to show up. But I wasn't tryna run up in this bitch by myself. Kong and Kiss were taking too long. I expected them to be here when I pulled up.

I jumped out the car, heading for Denver's steps.

"'Bout time your bitch ass showed up," Kong said as he and Kiss appeared out of the alley.

"Man, who house is this?" Kiss said, following me up the steps.

"Nevada's sister," I said.

"I can climb up to that second-floor window," Kong said, pointing at the window.

Kong didn't wait for the go ahead. He stepped onto the railing, Spider Man'd his way over to the top of the door ledge and jumped up, grabbing the windowsill. The nigga's upper arm strength was crazy. He pulled himself up, standing on the small ledge. One back kick and the window caved in.

"I be down there," he said, disappearing behind the curtains.

"It's quiet as shit in there," Kiss said. "Fuck that." Kiss walked down the steps, finding a rock. I went to fling it at the window when the front door opened.

"Ain't nobody in this bitch," Kong said at the door.

"You checked the whole house?" I stepped inside.

"I checked what I could check on my way to let y'all in this bitch. I ain't walk through this motherfucker like I was about to fuck something, but I'm telling you ain't nobody in this bitch." Kong tossed his arms up.

"Yeah, I said outside that it was quiet as a motherfucker."

"Help!" Denver screamed from the backyard.

We all rushed through the kitchen but, only me and Kong made it onto the deck. Kiss was out of sight. That nigga Vince was hanging Denver's ass over the balcony by her throat. I moved my arm in front of Kong to stop him from moving closer to the nigga. I knew what he wanted to do. He wanted to beat the nigga's ass. I wanted the same, but niggas had to be smart. Any move towards him and he was going to drop Denver. First instinct is always to protect your face.

"I told you to stop playing with me, bitch," Vince whispered forcefully in her ear. "You think you better than me? If I had the daddy you had, I'd be living just like you. You just got lucky. That luck just ran the fuck out. I wonder what will take you first —the pills, the fall, or me choking your ass the fuck out!" Vince screamed.

I heard of nigga's being jealous of a bitch. This was my first time seeing how wild that shit could get. Denver's struggle stopped, and she went limp.

"Denver!" We all whipped our necks around to the sound of Nevada's voice. "No!" Nevada screamed.

Turning back around, Vince had dropped Denver.

"You niggas tryna sne—" Vince started to talk, but Kong charged at him.

One hit stumbled his drunk ass. The second hit sent him to the floor of the deck. Nevada tried to run to the porch railing, but I grabbed her from behind. I didn't know what was waiting for her on the ground. Denver looked dead before she even hit the ground.

"Let me go!" Nevada yelled, trying to get out of my grip.

"Go in the house," I told her, pushing her inside.

I let her go, and she took off running to the basement. Chasing behind her, I couldn't keep up. Her adrenaline was giving her superpowers. She opened the back door and stopped.

"She ard," Kiss said, pacing the backyard with a cigarette. "This was under her tongue," Kiss showed us a pill before tossing. "She ain't swallow it."

Denver was on the grass, stretched out like she was getting the best sleep of her life. I couldn't wait to be on the way home to do the same thing. This had been the longest day of my life.

"Put your hands up!"

We couldn't see the police, but we saw the lights from their flashlights bouncing all around as they were running in our direction. I don't know who called them but even if it had been one of us, I didn't feel any safer. Me, Kiss, and Nevada stood with our hands up. Our best bet to getting out of this was for Denver to stay sleep. She could've woke up defending Vince. That's how these bitches did most of the time. They didn't leave until they were ready, even when they called for help.

Just my luck, Denver started coming to as the officers entered the backyard. Two of them went straight to Denver while one went to Kiss, putting cuffs on his wrists.

"The suspect is up there on the deck," Nevada told them.

"These two and the guy up there came to help my stupid ass sister. They didn't do shit wrong."

"Ma'am, are you alright?" one of the officers asked Denver.

"No," she said weakly. The other officer by her side called for an ambulance over his radio. "Why are you arresting him?" she asked. "He caught me when my boyfriend dropped me over the deck," she admitted.

"Thank God," I mumbled, relieved that we weren't on our way to jail.

The officer let Kiss out of the cuffs. He rubbed his wrists like them bitches had been on for hours.

"Thank you," Denver said to him. "Thank you to all y'all." She looked around.

"It won't happen again," Kiss said, sparking another cigarette.

And he meant that shit. He had a cousin that we saved one time. That bitch told us we beat her nigga too bad. Kiss said he would never help her ass again, and we hadn't since.

The police wanted statements from all of us. They managed to get two. One from Denver before she left with the ambulance. And the other from Nevada after she made sure her sister was safely in the ambulance. I walked out front with Kiss when Kong announced he was leaving.

"Aye, thank y'all for sliding." I dapped the both of them up.

"You already," Kiss said.

"You know a nigga always down to do some Kong shit. Especially since I'm a nine to five man now and a daddy after that. Shit felt good." Kong shook his shoulders, laughing.

"I catch you niggas later," I said, as Nevada appeared from the backyard.

"Wait," Nevada called out to them, jogging over. They stopped where they stood.

"Thank you." She hugged Kiss and then Kong. "Y'all don't even know my sister, barely know me for real . I know y'all showed up on the strength of Ship, but thank you. When it comes time for me to return the favor, I'm there." She nodded her head. "And not on the strength of my nigga. I fuck with y'all."

"Ard, sis." Kiss made eye contact with Nevada for the first time, holding his hand out for dap.

"I guess you one of us now." Kong dapped her up next.

"Been," I said as Nevada snuggled up under my arm.

Kiss and Kong walked off towards Kong's car. Me and Nevada walked over to hers.

"You took Rhea to Peaches?" I asked her.

"Yeah." She nodded. "Mari, too." She laughed a little. "I called Jemari to go pick him up from over her place."

That was some wild ass shit to hear. My little family was coming together better than I expected. Shit was falling into place and for the first time, it didn't feel too good to be true. It felt like I was getting everything that I deserved.

I wanted to fuck the shit out of Nevada. But after saving Denver from her nigga, I wanted Rhea up under me. So, Nevada followed me back to Peaches's spot to pick Rhea back up. I was hoping all the traveling woke her ass up so she could ask me a million questions, and I could answer every one of them. I let Peaches know I was on the way. I didn't expect to see her and Jemari standing outside with red solo cups in their hands when I pulled up.

"What's all this?" Nevada asked with a smile and hand gestures as we joined the two of them on the sidewalk.

"Just getting to know each other." Jemari put his hands up with smirk. "Our kids gon' be around each other, our exes probably getting married soon. We might as well be friends," Jemari explained himself.

"Oh, now you just wanna be friends," Peaches said with a grin.

"Oop," Nevada said.

"I mean, I ain't want to put you out there, but if it's like that then yeah," Jemari nodded his head, "I'm tryna be more than friends." He bit his bottom lip.

Peaches took a sip of her solo cup, looking at Jemari seductively. I bust out laughing. I ain't know much about Jemari. And I didn't give a fuck what Peaches had going on. They were both adults.

"Excuse me," I moved past them, "I wanna grab my daughter," I said, opening the screen door.

"Tell Mari to come on. These two fitna be nasty, and I don't want him to hear nothing," Nevada said, getting into her car.

In Peaches's house, Mari sat on the couch, watching cartoons with an orange soda and some Cheetos.

"Ya mama said come on," I told him.

"Ard." He got straight up with his things and headed out the front door.

Rhea was in her bed, knocked out. She looked too peaceful to move, but I did anyway. I carried her in my arms to the front door. Jemari held it open, and Peaches ran over to open my back door.

"Thanks," I told her, as I snapped Rhea into her booster seat.

"No, problem. See you," Peaches said.

She led Jemari into her place. Nevada pulled out of the parking lot, and I was right behind her. I hadn't forgotten the lie Peaches told about Rhea's daddy still being around. It just seemed pointless to hold on to it. Nevada let shit go enough to let her child wait for his father there. Peaches let shit go to the point that she allowed Mari to wait for his father there. I had to be an adult and let it go, too. She knew not to play them custody games with me no more. With her having Jemari's attention, hopefully, she had better shit to do with her time.

Nevada

"Sis!" Kong called out to me. "Niggas is hungry, man." He rubbed his stomach, leaning over on the couch he and Kiss had just carried in from the moving truck.

"We gon' eat after we get everything moved in, bro," I told him for the fifth time.

It was January first, and most of us were hungover from the celebration the night before. I suggested we wait to move in until we had a full day of rest, but Ship refused to wait.

We had to wait two months for my lease to be up. Then we had to do a short three-month lease, which made the rent five hundred dollars higher, because we couldn't find a place that the both of us loved. Ship wasn't budging on having a man cave. I held us up because I desperately needed a master bathroom. And we needed at least three bedrooms while we were getting our credit in order to buy a house. It was at the point where I was going to let Ship have his man cave and say fuck my bathroom because I wasn't doing another three-month lease.

We found this house not too far from the kids' school. We were bordering Baltimore City and Baltimore County. Far enough from the madness in the city but not too far that I couldn't go grab a chicken box when necessary. I was in love with this spot. The owners said that if we stayed for five years and kept the place up, they'd be willing to sell to us. We weren't interested because a three bedroom wasn't going to be enough for the five kids we wanted.

Getting pregnant was still a struggle for us. I'd been obsessively checking every day. It got to the point where Ship was checking my accounts to make sure I wasn't buying pregnancy tests or ovulation trackers.

"Damn," Peaches said, as she and Jemari walked into the house. "We early?" she asked.

"No, we're behind because these niggas have to take smoke breaks each trip from the old house to the new house," I told her.

Me and Peaches had long let go of our issues. But damn, if it didn't sting to see her pregnant. She was three months and showing already. It happened so fast for them. The shit wasn't fair. They met through us and not only had a baby on the way but moved in together.

I was happy that Jemari finally found someone to settle down with. The girlfriends in and out wasn't good for my son. I was even happy for Peaches. She fucked up so bad with ship, I knew she would never go out sad like that again. And not for nothing, she was loyal. Jemari would praise her for that. I think he put his cheating ways behind him because Mari hadn't mentioned any other women outside of Peaches. It could be the nigga was just moving smarter.

Ship came up behind me, wrapping his arms around my waist. He kissed on my neck. I brought my shoulder to my ear because he was on my spot.

"I can't wait to have that pussy in my face tonight," he whispered in my ear.

"I can't wait to feed you," I told him, turning around to face him.

"How you feeling, Big Ship?" I asked with my arms around his neck and my hands gripping the back of his head.

"Like the luckiest nigga in the world. You can't tell me I

ain't hit the mega millions." He laughed.

"It's not luck," I told him, staring into his eyes. "Luck is for mediocre. You great, baby." I kissed his lips. "And great men are blessed men. Your blessings are just catching up to you, that's all," I assured him.

Ship never gave himself enough credit. I made it a point to remind him what I thought of him. Even in moments of being frustrated with him, I was never unsure. I knew who my man was. I knew who he wanted to be. His every thought included the kids and me. This was the man that I wanted to come home to for the rest of my life.

"And the blessings started the day you smoked with me." Ship kissed me again. "We gotta do this last run to the old house, and then we'll be back. Have that food ready," he told me as he left me unpacking boxes labeled for the kitchen.

Food was already handled. I just hoped he wouldn't hate me when it arrived.

"Get on and sit y'all asses down somewhere," Ms. Ada barked orders at Mari and Rhea as she came in the house. "When do these little motherfuckers sleep?" she asked.

Me, Jemari, and Peaches laughed, greeting her with our own hugs. We all watched our language around the kids, but she wasn't going for it. Her exact words were, "I done lived too long to have you motherfuckers telling me what to do. I love y'all and I love them, but this is how Grandma talks, and them babies know that. They can't even say heck instead of hell or shoot instead of shit around me. Back in my day, the elders cursed, and we knew better than to repeat it out in the street. Well, around other adults because I was a cursing somebody."

We collectively decided to let her do her thing. She did keep it down to a minimum but after a day with the kids, she was always turned up a notch. I always offered to pick Mari and Rhea up after she spent some time with them, but she wanted them to stay the night. She said they kept her young. I didn't mind because she kept me kid free on the weekends.

Ms. Ada driving herself over with the kids said that TJ wasn't coming. I was disappointed about that. Ship, on the other hand, wouldn't care. TJ stayed with Amiyah after we told her about what happened on the show. She even moved in with her. But since the *Smoke with Me* episode hit YouTube, TJ hadn't been coming around. She wasn't returning Ship's calls or mine.

I'd been keeping tabs on her ass through social media. It was obvious that she and Amiyah had broken up. I reached out to her, in hopes that she'd show up today. I guess she was embarrassed. Hopefully, she'd get over it soon because Mari had been asking about her.

The doorbell rang, and I knew it was the chef. I rushed to the door to let her in. The dining room was the first room I set up. This would be our first dinner as a family, and I wanted all of us here. Schetta was coming by later with Saint and Whit after Whit got off of work. I also hadn't met Cambria, but she and Kiss hadn't been speaking. To my knowledge, she was just dropping the kids off to him with no words.

Ship said something about her getting an abortion. That's all I needed to hear to know that they were done. I'm not sure if Kiss knew that yet, though. While all of us were in committed relationships, he was single. And he seemed to be okay with it. Although, nothing ever seemed to rattle him.

"Hey, welcome, welcome," I said, opening the door.

"Nevada, right?" I nodded my head to confirm I was the same woman she saw with Patty, as she called Ship, in the restaurant.

Nadine tried to maintain her smile, but I could tell it was a struggle. Ship hadn't mentioned her since seeing her at the restaurant. But when I saved her number in my phone that night, she popped up in my "people you may know" section on Instagram. I saw that she had a small catering business. The reviews were always great.

Ship was going to be a little upset with me for intervening. But I hoped the excitement from everything else was going to drown out his anger with me.

"You can come in," I waved her in.

"Are you sure this is a good idea?" she asked.

"Yes. This is my home, and I'm inviting you in. Plus, I already paid you, so you kind of don't have a choice," I joked.

At the sight of a small smile, I forced her into a hug. I doubted Ship would be as welcoming, but I wanted her here. Ship shared some of the things he'd been through with Nadine. Most of those traumas were healed with him being a father. Then more with finding his grandma and his sister. Even the bullshit convos he had with his dad once a month did something for him. I knew in my heart that Nadine being around, even if just for the kids, would do Ship some good.

"Thank you for this." She gave me a tight squeeze. "But does Patty know I'm here?" She twisted her lips at me.

"Well, I'll be damned," Ms. Ada said, staring at Nadine.

"How are you doing, Ms. Ada?"

"Not as good as you, apparently. You look good. You off that stuff?" Ms. Ada asked, making everything in the room stop except the kids.

"Yes, ma'am," Nadine said proudly.

"Good to hear." She nodded her head, going back to her game of solitaire.

I led her into the kitchen so she could get set up. She

unzipped her luggage, pulling out pots and pans. She caught my attention as I was leaving her to do her thing.

“You never answered my question.” Nadine raised her eyebrows at me.

“No. Ship doesn’t know you’re here. If it’s a problem for him, I promise he’ll take it up with me, not you,” I assured her.

“I don’t want to be a problem. Especially not in his relationship. I imagine his dating life hasn’t been easy with all the mommy issues I’ve given him. And you seem to love him to do all this. I think it’s best that I go. I will text my assistant right now and have her come do the job.”

Nadine pulled her phone out and quickly pressed buttons. Her phone shook in her hand.

“You don’t have to be scared of him,” I told her. “He’s not that type of man. He’s calm, patient, he doesn’t let much get to him. He handles pressure with grace.”

“He sounds like a good man,” Nadine said.

“He is.” I nodded.

Nadine’s phone chimed and she looked at it. “My assistant says she’ll be here in thirty minutes.”

“Please, stay,” I asked her.

Before she could accept or decline my request, Peaches walked into the kitchen with Rhea on her side. When I first witnessed how often Peaches or Ship carried Rhea around, I thought they were doing too much. She was too big for that. But the more she warmed up to me, the more it became instinct to carry her. Maybe that’s just what little girls did.

As bad as I wanted a kid with Ship, I was hoping for another boy. I wanted to give Ship his first son but more than that, I didn’t want to steal Rhea’s spotlight. She’d have an easier time adjusting to a little brother than a little sister.

"Hey." Peaches smiled. "I'm Peaches, Ship's baby mother. And this is Rhea, your granddaughter. Rhea, this is your grandmother," Peaches said.

"Another one?" She asked excitedly, making us all laugh.

"Yes," Nadine nodded, "another one."

Rhea had met both my sets of parents. The four of them fell in love with her as quickly as I had. Peaches had taken her to meet Jemari's mama as well. She wasn't overwhelmed by any of it. In fact, she loved meeting new people now. We couldn't take her anywhere without her talking to strangers. Ship hated it, but she was just coming into her little personality.

"Peaches, put that damn girl on her feet," Ms. Ada gave orders, coming into the kitchen.

While we were trying to let our kids stay kids for as long as possible, Ms. Ada was from the old school. She promoted independence as early as possible. She said that our only job as parents was to prepare them to survive without us. It was the grandparents' job to spoil. And the great grandparents' job to instill the wisdom beyond their understanding.

By the time the boys got back, dinner was almost done. Schetta's six months pregnant ass was on the couch, directly in front of the fan. She tried to get me to turn the A/C on but in the middle of Winter, that was a dead request. None of my parents were here because they spent the holidays on separate vacations on separate islands. I invited my sister, too, but she'd been staying to herself ever since she got back with Vince.

I hadn't warned Ship that his mother was in our kitchen. Kong noticed her first because his greedy ass walked from the front door straight into the kitchen.

"Where the food at, sis?" Kong walked into the kitchen,

rubbing his stomach.

"It's almost done," Nadine said, wiping her hands on her apron before turning around to face us. "Well, look at you," she sighed, looking at Kong. "How you doing?"

"Lady, you don't know me," he said.

"I gave you your nickname because you used to climb up my fire escape like a damn ape." She raised her eyebrows, putting one hand on her hip.

"Hell nah." Kong looked in disbelief. "You look like a whole different person. How you doing, ma?" He leaned in for a hug.

"I'm good, baby. How's ya mama doing?" she asked.

"She good. She good. What you in here cooking?" Kong began looking at everything on the stove.

As she named everything that was cooking, Ship came in and stood against the wall. If I didn't feel someone burning a hole in the back of my head, I wouldn't have noticed him there.

"Bro, you ain't tell me ya mama was around," Kong said, eating a biscuit that Nadine passed him.

"Hey, Patty," Nadine said, now unsure of herself.

"Nadine has a catering business. She's trying to get it off the ground. I saw the reviews on her food and knew I had to taste it," I explained to him before he asked.

"Smells good," he said plainly.

He nodded his head for me to follow him. I excused myself and followed him down to the basement. Nothing was down here yet except the sectional. Ship took a seat, grabbed my hand, and sat me in his lap. He didn't say anything for a few seconds; he just looked at me. It was as lovingly as it had always been. I wasn't sure if he was mad.

"You mad?" I asked him.

"Moe to the, E to the," he sang.

We both bust out laughing from him singing the *Moesha* theme song.

"I was prying from a good place, I promise," I defended myself.

"You ain't ever gotta convince me of that. I know your heart, so I know your intentions. That's why I ain't trippin'." He shrugged.

"So, why we down here and not upstairs with everybody else?"

"A nigga been ripping and running all day. Just wanted a second with you."

I held Ship's face in my hands, kissing him like it was our wedding day. When he would say he was going to marry me, I never took it literally. But I knew now that he meant every word. I'd already started planning the colors.

Ship

"Ard, we about to get out of here." Peaches and Jemari stood from the couch.

"Daddy, can I stay with you?" Rhea asked.

"Not tonight, baby."

I stretched her arms out to give her some love before she left. Nevada had gone all out for a nigga and I was putting dick up in her tonight. The type of dick I was giving would require a kid free home.

"If she going, I want to go, too. Can I come with you, dad?" Mari asked his father.

"If it's cool with your—"

"It's cool!" Nevada hurried to cut Jemari off.

She was on the same shit I was on. I was putting a baby in her ass tonight.

"Bye, daddy." Rhea gave me a kiss and a hug, before climbing out of my lap.

"See you, Ship." Mari dapped me up before they both said their goodbye's to Nevada.

Peaches and Nevada hugged, while Peaches tossed me the peace sign as I dapped Jemari up. I didn't hate her ass no more but I liked Jemari more than I liked her. The way she played with me was still sitting on my chest. I'd get over it eventually. For now, the peace sign was more than enough.

"That's everybody except Nadine." Nevada said, shutting the door behind them as they left. "I'm going to take a shower." she kissed my cheek before jogging up the steps.

Nevada didn't have to verbally say she wanted me to talk to Nadine, yet she left enough context clues. It wasn't that I wasn't talking to her, a nigga just ain't have shit to say. I wasn't a man of many words – I ain't really know what words I wanted to give to her. I just knew that I wasn't mad at her and I didn't hate her no more. However, a nigga ain't feel ecstatic that she was around either. Maybe if I hadn't met G, TJ and Nevada. It was too late for me to care about that shit.

"You ain't gotta wash those dishes," I said walking into the kitchen. "You can just pack your stuff up and go."

"Is that your way of telling me that you want me to leave?" Nadine asked.

"If that's what I was saying, I would've just told you to get the fuck out." I assured her.

"Well in that case, I'll just finish up these dishes; if you don't mind,"

"Do your thing." I tapped the wall ready to head out of the kitchen.

"Patty," she called out.

I turned around, raising my eyebrows for her to talk.

"Are you never going to talk to me?"

"I just said mad sentences to you." I argued.

"You know what I'm talking about. You're a grown man now, and I respect you. I want to respect your wishes, too. I don't want to force myself on you; but I must say, I've grown so attached to Rhea in that short amount of time. I'd like to continue seeing her. You, too. Even Nevada, and everyone else that was here today. I want to be a

part of your life. But only if it's okay with you." Nadine lifted her eyebrows waiting on my response.

I thought I didn't care if she was here or not. However, hearing her say that she would disappear with the snap of my finger like a nigga was Thanos or something, had me feeling a way. I wasn't bothered by her being around nor did I look forward to seeing her, but I did get a rush of sadness at the thought of her not coming around. Still, I hadn't managed to respond so she continued.

"If it's fine that I'm around and you just don't want to talk to me right now, that's cool, too. But is it a right now thing or a forever thing? I know I don't have the right to put demands on you for anything, not even answers, but I would like to know how to move so I don't overstep with you."

"You cool." Was all I could manage to say.

"Good." She smiled. "Do you want to get the 'why' out of the way?" she asked.

"I already know why." I told her. "Look, I ain't really tryna go digging through my past – a nigga happy. Like the real kind. We get to digging up too much and that might change." I paused. I didn't want to be too harsh with my words but I wanted to be real with her. "We can start from here. Clean slate. I get to know you, you get to know me. We ain't gotta talk about none of that other shit. At least not right now, anyway."

Truth was, one day I might want to know about the grandparents, aunts and uncles I may have had; I couldn't predict the future. But right now, for the first time ever, a nigga wasn't chasing after shit. That emptiness in me had been filled. I was putting a lid on that motherfucker and sealing all this shit right where it was. We could work through the past later.

"Well, I have a daughter and I'm engaged." Nadine started off, showing me her ring.

The sound of my phone ringing snapped me from my

thoughts of Nadine.

"What's up, Pat?" I answered the phone for our monthly call.

"I ain't got shit going on, just seeing what's up with you. You busy?" he asked.

"Nah, just waiting on the people to call my name," I told him. "How was your weekend?"

I hadn't adjusted all the way to talking to Pat. We been doing this for a few months, and I still didn't know what to say to him for real . Nevada told me to use this time to just get comfortable, so I was rolling with it. I never called, never led the conversation either. Answering the phone was the only effort I put into it. I wouldn't even respond to what he was saying if a response ain't come to the top of my head.

"My weekend was good. Took my ol' lady out for a night on the town. Hopefully, she shut up about never going nowhere for a while." He laughed. "You know how these women can be."

"That's why you take them out before they start complaining," I told him.

Pat should have been the one giving me advice but more times than not, I was telling him how to be a man. Shit like "bills come first, then your pleasures". He should've known that already.

"You can come on in, Patrick." A nurse stood in the doorway to the back offices.

"Ard, Pat, I gotta take care of something. I'll talk to you," I said, ending the call before he could respond.

The nurse led me into one of the many offices in the back. She instructed me to take a seat in one of the two chairs across from her seat on the other side of the desk. A nigga was nervous as shit.

"So, everything looks great. I don't see anything that would suggest there being an issue with your sperm. They're strong and moving with intent. I know when you first came in, you said you hadn't talked to your wife about this. I think it may be time." She pursed her lips.

"Thank you for your time," I said, leaving out.

Nevada and I had been trying for months to have a baby. The shit wasn't happening. I was starting to wonder if I was the problem. When I sat down and thought about it, Peaches and I did a lot of raw fucking. Even if Rhea wasn't mine, she should've gotten pregnant again. But she was on birth control. I just had to clear my curiosity.

Hearing that my nut was swimming like it was supposed to put me in a fucked up position. I could tell Nevada that maybe she should have a doctor check her fertility and give her the same worries that I had. Or, I could just keep trying, knowing that it might not ever happen for us. I wanted to go into tonight's get together with a clear conscience. All I had done was remove one worry for another. Tonight was supposed to be perfect.

"Hey, here he goes," Nevada's dad, Lennox announced my arrival to her stepdad, Grant.

"And dressed the part, too. Check you out," Grant laughed, pulling me in for a hug.

Lennox and Grant lived on the green. Every Sunday morning, they were on the golf course. All they talked about is retiring, so they could travel all over the country for tournaments. They'd been trying to get me to come out and join them for a while. I'd been working so much overtime that when I finally did get a day off, a nigga ain't want to do shit but sleep, for real . I made time today, though.

"Y'all's daughter had this sitting out on the bed for me when I got in from work." I laughed. "How you doing?" I dapped Lennox up before hugging him, too.

"Can't complain," Lennox said.

"She first day of school'd you huh?" Grant thought the shit was hilarious. "Son, I been married for a long time, and my wife still *picks my clothes out for me."*

"Mine, too," Lennox chimed in.

I took this as the perfect opportunity and pulled my phone out.

"What else should I be prepared for when I ask Nevada to marry me?" I asked them, recording the two of them.

I could have never prepared myself for their reaction. You couldn't tell me they weren't watching the Ravens win the Superbowl. I could feel how happy they were.

"If this is your way of asking for my baby girl's hand, hell yeah." Lennox dapped me up. "Hell motherfucking yeah." He nodded his head.

"I couldn't have picked a better man." Grant gave me a firm handshake.

"And it's about damn time. Every time we see you, my wife wants to know if you asked me for Nevada's hand in marriage yet. The woman is working my nerves so bad, I'm thinking about renewing our vows," Lennox said, hitting the ball down the field.

"You got to watch out for him, Ship. The man is trying to steal your thunder." Grant joked with his beer.

"You better get to Nevada first because I'm going all out. Fancy ass anniversary ballroom party. Gonna start the night off with asking her to marry me again. I'm getting down on one knee, buying a new ring, the whole nine yards, man," Lennox filled us in on the details.

I hadn't even gotten that far. I didn't know how I was going to propose, only that I was. A nigga ain't know when or where. And now I had to rush to beat Lennox or make a bigger move than him, and I didn't have nowhere near that man's money.

That was weeks ago. I realized Lennox wasn't actually racing me. He was rushing me. I had to do this shit in my own time, though. I wanted the shit to be perfect. When Anton called saying he wanted to do an update episode, I jumped on it. Me and Nevada's *Smoke with Me* episode had been doing numbers. Motherfuckers were in the comments asking us to be a YouTube couple. Nevada really wanted to do it, but I told her ass no. I had enough of the cameras. I could give it one last go for her, though.

When I made it in the house from the doctor's appointment, Nevada was vacuuming the living room.

"Don't you walk through my living room with them shoes on. Take them off at the door." She pointed at the new shoe rack that wasn't there this morning.

"Let me find out you fitna be acting brand new for these cameras." I twisted my lips up at her.

"And am. And don't give a fuck either. Social media will zoom in on everything they can to find something to clown. Won't be us. Plus, this is the first time *Smoke with Me* is doing an update. Like, we have to set the standard."

On the drive over, I decided that I would tell Nevada I went to get checked, and my swimmers were swimming. I'd put it in her hands as to whether or not she wanted to check on her eggs. But now would not be the moment. I was going to give it until after the engagement. If a month passed and she still wasn't pregnant, then I would tell her. But I had to say something. One of the warnings that Grant gave me was to be upfront with her. Even if I felt like I would get in trouble. I wanted to go into this marriage doing the right thing.

"You not wearing that, are you?" Nevada turned the vacuum off and started rolling the cord up.

"What's wrong with what I got on?" I asked, scrunching my

face up.

"That's the same white tee and jeans you wore on the day we filmed the show. We wanna give progress, baby. I got something out for you on the bed," she said, disappearing into the kitchen.

"I bet you do," I mumbled.

Lennox gave me some advice that day, too. Pick my battles. Whatever she had laid out on the bed was something that was already in my closet. It wasn't a big deal to change into something that would make her happy. I did a quick change and just as I was about to make my way down the steps, my phone rang. It was Grandma so I couldn't ignore it.

"Hey, G." I answered the FaceTime, calling her by her new nickname.

"Did she say yes?"

"I ain't asked her yet." I laughed a little.

A nigga never cared to know what other people thought for real; but having the people I loved the most, not just support me proposing to Nevada, but be genuinely excited about it, had me feeling good.

"Well, shit. You might as well wait for me to get back home, then." G scrunched her lips up.

"You gonna be gone for another five days; I'm asking her today,"

G was in Jamaica with TJ. I still hadn't talked to my sister myself but Rhea saw her at G's the other day. Nevada asked Rhea how TJ looked and Rhea said she was big as a house. I'm sure she hadn't gained that much weight, but a heartbreak would do that shit to you.

"Well, shit, that's all I called for. Here, talk to your sister."

G's face disappeared and TJ's appeared, looking as disinterested as I felt. I wasn't mad at her ass; she was mad at me for whatever reason. I went to the last person in the world for advice about how to handle her. Kong said his sisters did that shit to him all the time. He told me that TJ would come around in her own time and to just pretend she never disappeared on me.

I wasn't that nigga. That shit bothered the fuck out of me. TJ and I were still playing catch up on all the time we lost. For her to just stop taking a nigga's calls was fucked up. I missed her more than I wanted to admit. Seeing her face on that screen did a nigga some good.

"Hey, I know we haven't talked," TJ started, running her hands down her face. "that's on me. I was going through some shit – still am. I'm hoping this island will get me right. When I get home, I'mma come see you. So, we can talk."

"I'm gonna talk and you gon listen. Then, you can talk." I told her.

"You know I'm the oldest right?"

"That we know of. Pat might have fifty-leven more kids out there somewhere."

The both of us burst into laughter. I hadn't known TJ that long but it legit felt like she'd been my annoying older sister forever. For the first time in my life I understood the phrase *lil-big sister*. She was older but she acted more like my lil sister; I was still supposed to be her protector and corrector. She'd never admit it but she wanted that.

The doorbell rang and I knew my time was up.

"Aye, I gotta go. I'll let y'all know what she says. And have some fun, not too much, though. You know G will leave your ass wherever you pass out at."

"Hell yeah." She laughed in agreement. "Love you, bro. I

know she's going to say yes so congratulations in advance!"

"Thank you, sis. Love you, too." I ended the called.

Making my way down the steps, I could hear Nevada greeting Anton and his camera guy at the front door.

"So, we can do this right here in the living room," she told them as I came down the steps.

"Ship! What's good, man?" Anton came over to dap me up. "I told you that shit was going to do numbers."

"You did, you did." I nodded my head. "How you been?" I asked.

"I'm good, man. I'm trying to hear what y'all got going on."

"Well, let's get the camera rolling," Nevada said.

I sat on the couch, and she snuggled up under my arm like we were about to watch a movie. Anton stood next to his camera man asking us questions. I let Nevada do all the talking. I was planning to end this shit with me doing my big one.

"We moved in a few weeks ago," Nevada answered Anton's question about our place.

He asked a lot of questions about the families blending. Shit that was on social media. And how it was adjusting to being in a relationship.

"Alright, one last question and I need both of you to answer. What advice do you have for others coming on *Smoke with Me*? If they want to get where the two of you are, what would you tell them?" Anton asked.

"Definitely go in with your shit in order. The biggest adjustment we had was getting on one accord with my daughter's mother. I was hesitant with certain shit that I should've had an understanding on before coming on the show," I answered, ready to get to my big one.

"I would say have an open mind," Nevada added. "I almost turned around in the parking lot. Then, I started planning on him choosing someone else once I saw all the other girls. Just be yourself, really." Nevada shrugged. "And let it flow. Don't force or fight it."

"Thank y'all so much for y'all time. Oh, I have one last question. The fans want to know if we'll be getting a baby soon," Anton cheesed, waiting on an answer.

The cameras wouldn't be able to tell, but my baby was panicked. She didn't want to tell the world that we'd been trying for months. It was something she'd been explaining to our family and friends. Everybody wanted us to have a kid. It got so bad, I had to pull motherfuckers to the side and tell them to stop asking her about that shit. That pressure wasn't doing shit but making it harder on us.

"I believe the phrase is first comes love, then comes marriage," I said, standing and pulling the ring box from my pocket.

I got down on one knee in front of a crying Nevada. "Baby, I don't think I'll ever have the words to express how much you mean to me. You really came into my life and flipped that motherfucker right side up. If I think about our future and you going first, a nigga can't breathe for real . I ask God every day that when he decides it's the end of the road for us that he takes me out of here. You superwoman 'round here to our kids. And you superwoman to me, too. That Lyfe Jennings song, "Must Be Nice", used to be true for me. I'd see the ride or die couples, dying to know when it was my turn. The moment I met you, I knew. I want to do life with you. Will you marry me?" I asked.

"Yes, baby." Nevada swung her arms around my neck, kissing me with her tear-stained lips.

I never doubted that she'd say yes. Still, the shit felt unreal. A nigga never planned on marrying nobody. Nevada had come out of the blue and had been my good luck charm since. I couldn't wait to see what the rest of forever looked like.

THE END

If you'd like to know more about Kong and Schetta and/or Ship and Peaches, you can find them in the standalone *Heavy is the Head That Wears the Bounty*.

If you'd like to know more about Ship and Poppie, you can find Poppie and Ship's quick appearance in the reality tv standalone *Pretty Robots*.

WANT TO INTERACT WITH T'ANN MARIE & HER TEAM? JOIN OUR READERS GROUPS ON FACEBOOK!

T'ANN MARIE PRESENTS: GRANDMA'S HOUSE | Facebook

BLACK AF URBAN BOOK LOUNGE | FACEBOOK

WIN PRIZES, BE APART OF LIVE
BOOK DISCUSSIONS & MORE!

Join Our Mailing List:

http://eepurl.com/gU81k5

GENRES:

- Urban Fiction
- Urban Romance
- Street Literature
- Urban Paranormal
- Interracial Romance
- Erotica

FOR CONSIDERATION, SEND THE FIRST 3 CHAPTERS OF YOUR MANUSCRIPT TO:

tannmariesubs@gmail.com

Made in the USA
Middletown, DE
14 December 2024